When Death Comes Stealing

"A DOZEN OR MORE
TOP-NOTCH WOMEN WRITERS
HAVE ROARED ONTO THE MYSTERY SCENE
IN THE LAST FIVE YEARS,
BUT VALERIE WILSON WESLEY
HAS HER SIGNAL LIGHT ON AND
IS ALREADY EDGING INTO THE PASSING LANE."

Margaret Maron,
EDGAR Award-winning author
of *The Bootlegger's Daughter*

"A STRONG NEW VOICE"

Detroit Free Press

"WELCOME PRIVATE INVESTIGATOR
TAMARA HAYLE!
A contemporary sister with bills to pay,
a son to raise, a life to lead,
and a heinous crime to solve.
WHEN DEATH COMES STEALING
is suspenseful and intelligent,
and crackles with wit and energy."

Jill Nelson, author of *Volunteer Slavery*

When Death Comes Stealing

A TAMARA HAYLE MYSTERY

VALERIE
WILSON WESLEY

AVON BOOKS ▲ NEW YORK

AVON BOOKS
A division of
The Hearst Corporation
1350 Avenue of the Americas
New York, New York 10019

Copyright © 1994 by Valerie Wilson Wesley
Excerpt from *Devil's Gonna Get Him* copyright © 1995 by Valerie Wilson Wesley
Inside cover author photo by Dwight Carter
Published by arrangement with G. P. Putnam's Sons
Library of Congress Catalog Card Number: 94-6597
ISBN: 0-380-72491-X

First Avon Books Printing: July 1995
First Avon Books Special Printing: April 1995

AVON TRADEMARK REG. U.S. PAT. OFF. AND IN OTHER COUNTRIES, MARCA REGISTRADA, HECHO EN U.S.A.

Printed in the U.S.A.

RA 10 9 8 7 6 5 4 3 2 1

Acknowledgments

I'd like to thank for their support and expertise my super agent, Faith H. Childs, my editor, Carrie Feron, the *Essence* crew: Joy Cain, Audrey Edwards, Angela Kinamore, LaVon Leak-Wilks, Benilde Little-Virgin, Ruth Manuel-Logan, Jill Nelson, Susan L. Taylor, Linda Villarosa, Diane Weathers, Barbara White, and as always, my husband, Richard.

To the memory of my mother,
Mary Spurlock Wilson

Oh, what you going to do
When Death comes stealing in your room?
O my Lord, O my Lord
What shall I do?

—TRADITIONAL

1

"Is that you, Tamara?" the voice on the phone asked.

I recognized him at once, but I didn't answer. DeWayne Curtis was the last person on earth I felt like talking to this Sunday morning, particularly since I hadn't even gotten out of bed.

"Is that you?" he asked again.

"Who the hell else do you think it is? You called my house, didn't you?" I finally said.

"I need to talk to you, Tamara. It can't wait. I'm in a phone booth down the Parkway."

"What?!" I screamed into the phone in disgust and propped myself up on my pillow. DeWayne Curtis's continuing assumption that I should arrange my life to suit his needs continued to enrage me. Fifteen years ago when I'd met and married him, I'd been young and foolish enough to think that his arrogant self-ishness was strength. I knew better now. "What do you want?" I asked with no pretense of politeness. Our son, Jamal, was in his room, presumably asleep, and there was no need to conceal my true feelings; I was free to talk to DeWayne as I pleased. "Say what you want and stay out of my life." I reached for a cigarette in the nightstand drawer where I used to keep them, forgetting that I'd stopped six months ago. DeWayne had that effect on me.

"I need to talk to you," he repeated, more urgently this time. "Something's gone down that I've got to talk to somebody about. I've got to come by, Tammy."

So it's Tammy now, I thought. *It must be serious.* He hadn't called me Tammy since I'd left him. I didn't say anything for a couple of minutes; I figured I'd let him wait. It was raining outside; even before I'd opened my eyes, I'd heard the drops hitting the pane on the skylight I'd put in last summer. It gave me a certain pleasure to think of DeWayne Curtis standing in the rain waiting for me to make up my mind. The only thing I'd really felt like doing this morning was lying in bed—undisturbed and peaceful—with nothing more taxing on my mind than whether I should brew a pot of that Blue Mountain coffee I'd brought back from my yearly splurge trip to Negril or give my caffeine-jones a break and make a cup of Red Zinger tea.

"Tammy," DeWayne said again. I sucked

my teeth. "Tammy, Terrence died yesterday. Terrence is dead."

"Sweet Jesus," I said and sat up. "Give me a few minutes to put some clothes on, De-Wayne, and come on by."

I hung up and sat there for a minute, thinking about what he'd just told me. I knew that it would be only a matter of time before that boy died, living the kind of life he'd lived, but I also knew what DeWayne must be feeling. He may have been a tired-ass son of a bitch when it came to women, but he loved and took care of his sons. It was the one and only thing I really respected about him. I knew this had hit him like nothing else could.

DeWayne had four sons by different wives, including Jamal, the one I'd given him. Except for Hakim, who at sixteen was the closest to Jamal in age, and the one I'd helped raise for the five years we'd been together, I didn't really know the others. I'd seen Gerard a couple of times; he was the one DeWayne had had by his white wife, Emma. I'd seen Terrence, the lately dead and the one by his first wife, even less. Terrence and Gerard were both losers as far as I could tell: Terrence messed with crack, and Gerard always had a nasty attitude and a nutty look in his eyes, like he'd as soon pull out an Uzi and waste you as nod hello. DeWayne's sperm must have improved with age; Jamal and Hakim were both turning out OK.

I tried to remember the last time I'd seen Terrence, but I kept drawing a blank. I could only remember him as a kid. The first time I'd met him, he'd come by our place the day I brought Jamal home from the hospital. He'd been a big-eyed eight-year-old who knew Delores, his mama, hated my guts but who'd brought his new baby brother a Grandmaster Flash and the Furious Five album and a bottle of apple juice anyway. He'd been awkward and skinny, and I couldn't see any of his daddy in him or tell if anything about him would look like my son. It's hard to say what will happen to a kid in a lifetime. I don't know when Terrence went bad and started messing with crack or why life had jerked him around like it had. But he didn't deserve to die at twenty-two years old—nobody does.

"Hey, Ma, can you give me a couple of dollars?" Jamal said, breaking into my thoughts as he bounded into my room and plopped down on my bed. He looked as if he'd shot up a foot over the summer, but he hadn't yet grown into his body. He moved like a baby giraffe, all legs and height, but he still had a kid's face that even the hint of a mustache didn't change. I could see my dead brother, Johnny, in him whenever I looked at him.

"We got to talk," I said. He read my eyes and worry flitted across his face.

"What happened?"

"Your daddy called a few minutes ago. Terrence died yesterday."

He didn't say anything, but his eyes filled with tears and he quickly glanced away so I couldn't see them. He saw his two oldest brothers maybe once, twice a year, but he always spoke of them with affection—imagining, I guess, the relationship he wished they had. De-Wayne's wives and the children he'd had by them lived out their lives in separate worlds from ours, but the worlds seemed to mesh for Jamal. To him, the blood-bond between him and his brothers was stronger for its absence.

"How did he die?" he asked without looking at me.

"Crack," I said. I didn't know that for sure, but I assumed that that was what had killed him. "Did your daddy tell you Terrence was doing crack?"

Jamal nodded. I never knew what DeWayne told him or didn't tell him, and I rarely asked. Their relationship was theirs, and I stayed out of it as much as I could. DeWayne was an asshole, and I only hoped that that simple truth would not hurt Jamal when he finally found it out as much as it had hurt me when I had.

I hugged him and held him tight, and he didn't try to break away. He had a man's body now, and the difference between that and the child's body he'd had a year ago shocked me for a moment. At fourteen, he thought himself a man and looked like one sometimes, but I could still see the boy. After a minute, he pulled away.

"Is the . . . the funeral going to be soon? I want to say good-bye." His voice cracked, the kid breaking through.

"Your daddy will be coming by in a few minutes, and you can talk to him about the arrangements he's made." He nodded and headed toward his room, and after a few minutes I heard Ice Cube's voice blasting from behind his closed door.

I pulled on some jeans and the Howard University T-shirt I'd bought the last time I'd been in D.C., and went into the kitchen to fix myself a pot of strong Jamaican coffee. Then I sat down at my kitchen table and stared out at the rain.

There are three things in this life I cherish: my independence, my son, Jamal, and my peace of mind. DeWayne Curtis had it within his power to mess with two of those. In the past few years, I've managed to clear my life of things that aggravate my spirit: I used to be a cop. Some might say I couldn't handle the shit I was supposed to put up with—being black, being a woman—and I guess that's about right. I knew who I was and I wouldn't let them change it. I quit five years ago and Hayle Investigative Services, Inc., was born. Since then I've changed lots of things. I used to smoke; I chew gum now. I gave up pork (except barbecued ribs on the Fourth of July), and I see as little of DeWayne Curtis as I can manage. But blood is blood, as my brother, Johnny, used to say. He died when I was twenty, which is probably why I married DeWayne at twenty-one. Grief will do that to you.

I'm in my thirties, too old to put up with anything or anybody that breaks my day. Yet DeWayne always seems to pop back into my life like the proverbial bad penny, and there doesn't seem to be a hell of a lot I can do about it. I can't deny my son his father. But my peace of mind is another matter, and that was what was at risk as I faced him over coffee this morning.

"I loved that boy, Tamara. I loved that boy. Why is it that everything always turns to shit? Why can't I be happy? Why does everyone I love leave?" He asked the questions all at once, and they flowed into each other in a weepy litany of self-pity.

I studied him for a minute without saying anything. He was as fine in his forties as he'd been in his thirties, and probably as he'd been in his twenties, but now he had money and attitude. He could charm the panties off a nun if he set his mind to it, and he knew it. Even this morning, in the midst of his grief, he looked like he'd just stepped off the pages of GQ. He had taken the time to put on a deep-gray, washed-silk shirt that fit his body like a glove and worked with his deep-gray charcoal trousers. His gold watchband glittered on his wrist in a flash of expensive subtlety. I glanced past him out my kitchen window and thought about how leaves on the big chestnut tree in my neighbor's yard were almost gone and how the lilac bush Jamal had planted by the front porch probably wouldn't make it to spring. I also noted the roof of his new silver Lexus glistening in the morning rain. When I glanced back at him, I noticed the tears in the corners of his eyes. I'd seen DeWayne Curtis in a lot of moods, but I'd never seen him cry.

"Want some more coffee?" I asked. He took some, and gulped it down. "I wish I could say something, DeWayne, except I'm sorry."

"Just letting me come here is enough, Tammy."

"Don't call me Tammy," I snapped. It had been his pet name for me when we'd been together, and the sound of it rolling off his lips for the fourth time this morning made me want to puke. He looked at me, surprised then hurt. I quickly looked away. It had taken me years to get over our joke of a marriage, and I didn't want to see any of his sudden vulnerability or feel any fake closeness.

"I didn't mean to say anything to offend you. I just meant it was nice of you to let me come by." He said it nastily, sarcastically; the DeWayne I knew.

"I didn't mean to snap," I said, backing

8

down. *The man was grieving, after all; I had the upper hand.* "But just don't call me Tammy."

"We *were* married once," he said pulling the old charm up from somewhere. "Those were some of the best years of my life."

I nearly choked on my coffee. He chose to ignore me and stared at the wall above my head for a moment. I sneaked a look at the clock. He'd been here for ten minutes, and I was ready for him to leave.

"Tam . . . Tamara," he said after a minute. "There's something I've got to tell you that I haven't told anybody else." The urgency in his voice caught my attention. "Terrence—wasn't the first one. He wasn't the first."

"The first what?"

"He wasn't the first one to die."

"What do you mean?"

"Just what I said," he said impatiently.

"What are you talking about?" I didn't mean to say it angrily but that was the way it came out, and I didn't change it. "DeWayne, what do you mean?"

"Listen to me, damn it, he wasn't the first one of my boys to die." He grabbed my shoulder more firmly than he probably meant to, demanding my attention with force. I pulled away angrily, but the despair in his voice startled me. "He wasn't the first one of my sons to die," he repeated.

He's in worse shape than I thought, registered somewhere in my mind.

"DeWayne, you have four sons," I said patiently. "You have lost Terrence. I know how terrible this is for you, and I grieve with you, but you have only lost *one* of your children, not two."

He looked at me, through me in disbelief. "I never told you about my boy in Virginia, in Salem, did I? He was down there and I was up here . . . I never told you about him."

Anger hit me, so deep I could almost taste it. *One more lie, just one more!* I thought, and then I was mad at myself for giving him the power to still hurt me. Lying came as easily to DeWayne Curtis as cursing comes to some men. Throughout our five years of marriage, he would lie to me about everything—from how much he'd paid for a bag of cookies to where he'd spent the night.

"So you have another kid?" I asked, pouring myself more coffee, avoiding his eyes. I took a sip, not allowing him to see through to my feelings. That was the one good thing that being a cop had taught me. I could lie with my eyes as easily as the coldest bastard who walked the streets. He answered slowly, his tone suddenly confidential.

"I was just twenty-two, trying to make it on my own. My first boy." His eyes shifted away from me, telling me I still wasn't hearing the whole truth, but I didn't want to press him. "The boy's mother was twenty. It was 1969. Liberation Times, but not down there, not in that town. A woman got pregnant, she had to have it. But there wasn't any love between us. Not like there was between you and me."

I let that one pass.

"But I did stay in touch with the boy, and she named him after me. She called him DeWayne."

"Did she have a name?"

"Willa. I sent him what I could, and at least he knew he had a daddy, although I wasn't a daddy like I was to the rest of my boys, I wasn't able to be. But he's dead now."

"When did he die?"

"A year ago. A year ago yesterday. The fourth day of October, Tamara. The same damn day as Terrence." A chill went through me. Life was definitely kicking DeWayne's ass. But I had heard of stranger things. During my years in the department, I'd seen so much shit without reason or rhyme it didn't even shock me anymore—one of the reasons I'd had to leave. Death, that ass-kicker who never takes a holiday, could knock on anybody's door whenever he felt like it, and DeWayne was no exception. Neither was I, for that matter. But maybe DeWayne was reaping what he'd sown.

"Tamara, something's happening. Something is happening to my kids and I don't know how to stop it."

"DeWayne, sometimes things just happen . . . it's been a year . . ."

"Why the same day like this, the same

damn day, exactly a year apart? I'm still mourning my first son, and then this shit happens, like somebody's telling me something I don't want to hear. Something is not right, Tamara, I know it. You know how good my instincts are. You know they're better than gold. It's a pattern somebody's throwing at me, kicking my ass with a pattern I can't see."

"There's no pattern, DeWayne. It's just a terrible coincidence. How did your first son die?"

"Shot. A hold-up, the cops said. He was coming home from work and somebody shot him dead."

"It's been a year, do they know who did it?"

"They picked up some kid a couple of months ago. They been holding him for trial. A boy not much older than Hakim. They say some of his friends told them that he was the one who did it. They say he had DeWayne Junior's wallet and car keys."

"And Terrence, how did he die? An overdose?"

He looked down at his lap. Maybe the shame of how his son had died, of how he had let him live, was hitting him for the first time. He looked old suddenly, and I knew how he would look as an old man, wrinkles creasing his face, no teeth.

"Yeah," he finally answered, head still bowed. "Tamara. Something isn't right about this. Those boys dying so young, my kids . . ."

"What's not right is that they were young,"

12

I said, "and that you loved them and that you're grieving for them like you've never grieved before." *And*, I thought to myself, *that your guilt is kicking in, how you treated their mamas and how you weren't there for them like you should have been. That's what's wrong with you.*

He started to cry, without any sound, the tears rolling down his face. Jamal came into the kitchen then and sat down next to him. I left them alone together and went into the living room, closing the kitchen door behind me, but after a few minutes, DeWayne came in and sat down beside me.

"Tammy, could you go to my boy's place and look around to see what you can find?"

His question caught me off guard. "There's nothing to find, DeWayne."

"Just go and look around. The cops thought he was just another junkie, that's all he was to them. They might have missed something. That boy was trying to stay away from coke. He hadn't done anything for two months. He was cleaning himself up. Something else killed him.

"I'll pay you for it, Tamara, I know you can use the cash. I'll pay you double whatever you charge, plus your expenses."

Despite myself, my interest picked up. Money, that was what made DeWayne tolerable. Money. It always came down to that. And he was right. I needed the cash. I was doing better than I had the first few years after I'd left the force, when everyone, including me, had told me I was crazy. Things had improved, but they were slow this month. Spring was my big season—men got the hots and started cheating on their women, and kids ran away to check out the world. Everybody was looking for somebody and willing to pay me to look. But nobody left home heading into winter. The few freelance cases the Public Defender's office shot me always seemed to dry up in October. I could definitely use some bucks.

Jamal came into the room and sat down beside us, his eyes and ears taking in everything we said. Then he glanced up at me, with a begging in his eyes the likes of which I hadn't seen since he'd been a kid and wanted something bad.

"OK, DeWayne," I said after a minute. "I'll go over to Terrence's place and see what I can find." Jamal gave me a look that said thanks, and I nodded back. *I'll do it for you*, I thought as I gave him a half-smile. *And for that skinny little boy who defied his mama's wishes and came to bring you his blessings.*

14

2

Newark is a survivor city—an old fighter who won't go down for the count. Johnny used to talk about how Broad Street stretched out—grand movie theaters, department stores, big-time musicians playing Newark *first*, and you couldn't make it down the streets on a Saturday night. But everything changed after the '67 riots.

I grew up in the Central Ward, the Hayes Homes. I was ten when cops beat up some cabbie right around the corner from where I lived, and word had it that they'd killed him. Newark folk, who don't take no shit, went into the streets. When things cooled, nothing was the same. All the money left, the big bucks and the little. My parents moved to East Orange a year later. But I'm a Newark girl at heart, always will be.

Things are coming back now, block by block rising from the ashes—like that Egyptian bird.

This city of mine has seen some hard times, but keeps climbing back, just don't know when to leave that ring.

During the Seventies, some of the best real estate was cheap for a hot minute, and that's when DeWayne got his lock on a spot on Branford Place. It had the look of money but the scent of decay still lingered.

He called me twice on Monday to cry some more about Terrence and the son I didn't know, so I promised I'd go over to Terrence's place on Tuesday morning and tell him what I'd found out after the service that night. I avoided his Branford Place office as much as I could. I was scared it would be just my luck that some fool DeWayne had suckered would wander in to put a bullet through his head, and one in mine just for being there.

I'd been here to pick up some money for Jamal a couple of months ago. DeWayne dealt in cash, never checks. He'd gone into a safe hidden behind a tacky picture, pulled out three hundred dollars in twenty-dollar bills and given them to me in a greasy McDonald's bag, which I'd tucked into my pocketbook in disgust.

In all the time I'd been with DeWayne, he'd never told me exactly how he made his money, but there always seemed to be plenty of it. In the first year of our marriage, I'd been too stupid to ask questions. In the last, I'd been too smart. The first thing I did after I got my

P.I. license was find out how to get the goods on people without them knowing it, and the first person I ran a check on was DeWayne Curtis. He owned a couple of clubs in East Orange and one in New Brunswick, and he was a silent partner in at least two small convenience stores in Newark's Central Ward. I'd heard that he was part of a group that handled stolen cars, and rumor had it that he and his boy Basil Dupre had their fingers deep in laundering money for the mob. But nobody could catch him. He was smart like a rat.

The smell of mildew floated up from the carpet as I walked into the lobby of his building. Water stains on the peeling asbestos ceiling formed dollar signs, reminding me why I was there.

The fifth floor hall, where DeWayne's office was, was deserted, and I moved quickly down the hall, but when I stepped in I stopped dead in my tracks. Last time I'd been here, it had looked as nasty as the lobby. The walls, covered with flowers the size of fists, had contrasted with the cheap red couch, which shared cigarette burns with the coffee table. But DeWayne had obviously come into some serious money. The place was now a soft, creamy color, and the chocolate-colored corduroy couch looked brand-new. Prints of collages by Romare Bearden and Varnette Honeywood tastefully dotted the walls. The new receptionist, who'd replaced the gum-smacking, weave-tossing, clunky-gold-earringed sister who'd sat in the spot last time I'd been here, definitely added some class.

"May I help you?" she asked, pronouncing each word as if she were rehearsing for a play. Her voice wasn't what you expected; it was a kid's voice, high and sweet, that didn't quite belong to her face. She was plumpish, what Johnny, my dead brother, used to call "healthy," and looked like she'd been raised on grits and fried country ham. Her frumpy gray suit made her look ten years older than I thought she probably was, but she was pretty in a way that didn't call attention to itself. Downhome pretty.

I wonder if he's fucking this one, I thought to myself. DeWayne usually found some way to get into the pants of pretty young things who worked for him, and even some of the not-so-pretty ones. I'd seen her pink silk blouse in Bloomingdale's a couple of weeks ago, and there was no way in hell that DeWayne could be paying her enough to afford it.

"Is Mr. Curtis in?"

"No, I'm afraid that he's not."

"Hi, I'm Tamara Hayle."

"I know who you are." Sister had a bit of an attitude. I decided to ignore it.

"Mr. Curtis told me to stop by for the keys to his, uh, his late son's apartment. Did he leave them for me?" As much as I can, I avoid mentioning my relationship to DeWayne to people who know him. The less said about past mistakes the better.

"Oh yes," she said, with a proper little nod. She reached into the drawer, pulled out a set of keys, and handed them to me. I noticed that the tips of some of her fingers were missing. I wondered if it was a birth defect or an accident. She caught me looking and folded her hand into a ball, placing it back in her lap.

"He said to tell you that the address is Two Forty-one Avon Avenue, here in Newark." *Neu-rirk,* she said it like some natives do, but I didn't think she was.

Avon Avenue had been grand back in the day, and it still had an elegant rich-folks-playing-in-the-garden ambience, but it had fallen on hard times. Now some of the older, larger places were boarded up and others had been turned into boardinghouses; a couple of the new residents were questionable, most perfectly respectable. Terrence had probably fallen into the former category. I glanced back at Ms. Receptionist, whose eyes had fastened back on her work. I wondered what she could be working on so hard that would require such concentrated attention.

"New here?" I asked after a minute, knowing she was.

"A couple of months," she said, glancing up, and then she looked back down at her work. "Actually, I've been here since May." She had a soft Southern accent that she tried to hide but that kept sneaking through on the ends of her words.

"DeWayne has really done some nice things with this place," I said, glancing around the office again, trying to make conversation. "Did he come into some money? Miss . . ." I paused, waiting for her to give me her name.

"July."

"Miss July."

"No, July is my first name."

"You were born in July?"

"No. October. My mama had a sense of humor."

We both laughed. I knew the accent now, it was country trying to sound city, and it touched something deep inside me—an insecurity that tries to hide itself, always striving to be better and not knowing you're fine just the way you are. Her laugh was girlish, self-conscious, and dimples creased her cheeks. I liked her smile.

"I'm ashamed of my name sometimes," she said shyly, not looking directly in my eyes, as if she were talking to someone on the other side of the room. I squelched an impulse to look behind my shoulder. "It sounds so country."

"With folks naming kids everything from Sermonetta Wailing to Penis Brown, July, no matter when you were born, is fine," I said reassuringly. "So where are you from?"

She looked up surprised, as if I'd become

too personal. The shield went up again.

"Around," she shrugged.

"Around here?"

"Florida," she finally said. "South Florida is where I grew up. Do you know which key opens which door?" she asked. I glanced at the keys.

"Shouldn't be too hard to figure out. There's only three." I held them up to show them in case she'd forgotten.

She was older than I'd thought at first, early thirties, maybe only a couple of years younger than me, but not old enough to be wearing that suit she had on. It was an older woman's suit, and it made me think about my aunt and how she had always tried to dress me after my parents died, until my older sister, Pet, had put her foot down and made her stop. It looked like something her mama had picked out—or that my aunt would have.

"So, when did the decorating start?" I asked, glancing around the office.

"Before I came," she said.

"Looks good."

"I wouldn't know. I never saw it before." *Dead end for that one, too.*

"OK, July. I'll be talking to you," I said, heading toward the door. Before I left, I turned to toss a parting comment. "Too bad the way that boy went out. He was a nice kid."

"For a junkie," she said. Her bluntness startled me, and threw me off-base for a half-minute.

"I thought things were finally working for him," I said. "Did he ever come around here?" I asked it on the spur of the moment, habit more than anything else. Old habits die hard and five years in this business had taught me that information always comes from the throwaway comment of a super or ambulance attendant or receptionist who has no secrets to keep or angles to cover.

July looked puzzled for a moment and then smiled a sad dimpled smile. "You mean Terrence?" she asked, then answered her own question. "He came up a couple of times to talk to DeWayne, but he never said too much to me, and before everybody knew it, he was dead. That's the way life is, I guess. Short and sweet." She said it casually like a thoughtless child delivering a zinger so cruel you want to slap her across the face.

Her eyes went back to her work, fingers in a ball, pencil in mouth. I was dismissed.

Hope he's not fucking this one! I said to myself as I left, realizing in the next thought that I didn't really care. My thoughts had turned to other things: the time it would take me to get to Avon Avenue, check out Terrence's apartment, pick up Jamal's suit from the cleaners, fix some dinner, and get us over to the wake and back home as soon as I could. No time. There was never enough.

And there was dealing with Jamal's grief. I knew he needed time to mourn. But I wanted his life to return to normal as quickly as it could. I wanted to protect him from those parts of DeWayne that frightened me—money from strange sources kept in fast-food burger bags, half-brothers who died before their time. Yes, we would go to the wake. Jamal would cry and mourn. DeWayne would pay me my fee for checking out Terrence's apartment, and then our lives would return to math tests, basketball games, lying in bed on a Sunday morning. The sooner all of this was over, the better. I glanced at my watch, turned the key in the ignition of my '82 diesel Jetta and in a cloud of smelly exhaust headed over to Avon Avenue to see what I could see.

3

It had been raining on and off since Sunday, and the drops started again as I headed toward Avon Avenue. The day had a chill to it, too damn cold for October, and the damp air that seeped into the cracked vent window of my Jetta made me think about money—the fact that I didn't have any.

The boardinghouse where Terrence lived loomed like a battleship at the edge of Avon Avenue. It was the biggest thing on the block—creepy, old and ugly, the kind of place kids throw eggs at on Halloween. Several large trees and overgrown hedges kept the sun from touching the house, and the old iron gate that surrounded it creaked when I opened it like something out of a horror movie.

I rang the doorbell twice, and when nobody came, I cautiously let myself in with the set of keys I'd gotten from DeWayne's office.

"Hello, anybody home?" I called as I en-

25

tered and nervously glanced around the foyer. You never know when some nervous fool is going to break bad and blow you away figuring you're a thief. I walked a few steps into the house. "Anybody home?" I yelled out again to the empty space.

The foyer was gray with a worn brown carpet, bits of floorboards peeking through in places. There were two decrepit umbrella stands filled with umbrellas of different sizes in various need of repair. A green glass vase filled with pink plastic roses on a credenza near the wall looked like it needed dusting. The four doors on the far end of the foyer were closed. The house had the damp, dark smell of a basement after the rain. Television voices droned somewhere, and music from a radio drifted down from the upper floors.

"What you want?" barked a low, croaky voice out of nowhere. I tensed. Whoever was speaking sounded like she had a .22 trained at the back of my head. I felt that quick rush of adrenaline I always feel when I'm surprised, and turned around to face a tiny old woman in a faded yellow nightgown, her round face the color and shape of a chestnut. She looked vaguely familiar, one of those faces you know you've seen somewhere but you don't know where or with who.

"What you want?" she asked.

"Sorry to disturb you," I said, trying my best to sound like I had a right to be standing in the middle of her foyer. "I'm Tamara Hayle. I'm a private detective. I've been asked by Terrence Curtis's father, DeWayne Curtis, to look into his son's death." I paused for a moment letting her take it all in. "I'd like to go into his—Terrence Curtis's room and look around, if that's possible?" I made it sound like a question rather than the statement it was.

"No, it's not possible," she said, examining me suspiciously. "Look in his room? What you looking in his room for? The boy dead. Bad enough he died here in my house without nobody coming to look in his room. Let the dead rest in peace. R-I-P. That's what I say."

She sucked her teeth in disgust, then started nodding her head, which was covered by a long blue-black wig that looked as if it had been put on in a hurry.

"The boy died. He dead. No sense in talking about it. No sense in looking in his room." She half-cocked her head and then looked at me again as if seeing me for the first time. "I'm Miss Lee," she said. "I own this place. What you want to know?" For a moment I wasn't sure if she'd heard me, was senile, or was just giving me a hard time.

"I'm Tamara Hayle," I started again. "A private—"

"You done told me once who you were and what you want. I'm just not sure if I want to let you into that boy's room without no police

27

here or nothing." She was definitely not senile. I decided to be straight with her.

"I've been hired to look into the death of Terrence Curtis. I used to be married to his daddy," I said formally, adding the part about my relationship with DeWayne as an after-thought. Her expression didn't change. "The boy, Terrence, was kin to my son, and I prom-ised his father and my boy I'd look into his death."

"Kin to his daddy? I know his daddy." The way she said it and the way she eyed me sus-piciously caught my attention, but I didn't fol-low it up. DeWayne was into a lot of things, and he knew a lot of people.

"Look, I just want to look around the room," I said. "See if there's anything that seems out of place. I won't be in there more than five or ten minutes. It's a special favor to his daddy."

She narrowed her eyes slightly. "The cops were here. They were here on Saturday when they took the boy out and they were here again yesterday, looking for nothing, and didn't find shit."

The "shit" startled me. It always surprised me to hear women over sixty curse, although I'll probably be one of them someday.

"I got to rent this place out again," she con-tinued. "It's bad enough the boy died here without you poking around."

"Ten minutes? All I need is ten minutes. I'm

not going to disturb anything in ten minutes. I'm really not here to bother anything. Nothing went down and I know that as well as you do." I gave her what I meant to be a reassuring wink and a pat on the arm. "I'm just doing this as a favor for his daddy. It's really not a big thing, believe me. Listen, this is my job. He's paying me." I emphasized the "paying." Money. One sister to another.

She studied me closely, her mouth in a thin tight line, running some options back and forth in her mind, which surprised me because it didn't really seem to be such a big thing. But some folks just don't like people poking around in their houses for no good reason, and maybe she was right. I was just about to tell her to forget it, to go back to her room, put her wig on straight, do whatever she was doing, and I'd go on my way to mind my own business, when I remembered the money.

"Ten minutes," I said again, putting a little beg in my voice.

"Ten minutes is all you got," she said, still eyeing me suspiciously. She reached in her pocket for a set of keys and headed up the stairs. I followed obediently, deciding not to mention that I had my own set since she didn't seem to care how I had gotten in.

The light that slipped in timidly through windows covered by ancient venetian blinds was dim, and Miss Lee snapped on a naked overhead bulb to light the stairs, which she

climbed two at a time. It was a cruel reminder
that I had to get my butt back to the gym. I
silently cursed my days of wine and Newports. The house was four damp and dusky
stories in all, about seventy years old, built in
the days before the white folks in Newark
starting running from the black ones. But
whomever the house once belonged to, it was
Miss Lee's now.

"This is a good house, a good house, and I
don't let no addicts in," she said, keeping up
a steady stream of conversation as we
climbed. "I can smell an addict sure as a
hound can smell a coon. And why that boy
would go and start messing with dope again
... There's no telling about people these days.
You can't tell nothing about nobody these
days ... you can't tell me nothing about nobody these days. Nothing ... When I found
that boy's body, I—"

"You found the body?" I asked, stopping
midstep. She looked at me as if she were surprised I didn't know.

"Yeah. He was playing his music too loud
that night. Saturday. He always played it loud
during the day, but this was ten-thirty at
night, and he knew my rules about playing
music at night, even on a weekend. Folks got
to get up and go to church on Sunday morning. So I came up here to tell him to turn it
down. And that boy wouldn't turn it down.
So I kept on knocking and finally I decided to

go in and turn it down myself. And when I came in, I seen he was dead. I called an ambulance."

"Where did you find him?"

"Laying 'cross his bed." She stopped climbing for a moment. I caught my breath. "I could tell the boy was dead the minute I laid eyes on him. His eyes was as flat as one of them fishes you get at the fish store, and he looked like he was made of wax. But I didn't want no cops in here so I called the hospital. But the cops came anyway. They said it was cocaine that killed him."

We started climbing again. "How long had Terrence lived here?"

"About two, maybe three months."

Terrence's room was the only one in the attic. She opened the door and stood back. "I hired some people to come in here and clean day after tomorrow, and everything is going. Tell his daddy if there's anything he want out of here he better come on by and get it."

"OK," I said. "Thanks."

"Ten minutes," she said again and closed the door behind her.

I stood for a moment in the sparsely furnished space and then walked over to the still unmade bed by the window where I assumed Terrence's body had been found. It seemed disrespectful to sit down; I'm squeamish about stuff like that. So I stood where I was and surveyed the room.

It was a long, rectangular room with small paneled windows, the kind of space you could snap some skylights in, stain the floor and charge some sucker three times what Miss Lee was getting. But the room had an eerie quiet to it, a place where somebody had fought demons and lost.

The sheets and pillowcases were clean, and there were several cassette tapes—Toni Braxton, John Coltrane's *Ballads*—lying on top of what looked to be a secondhand portable tape deck. I turned on the deck, and Trane's "I Wish I Knew" began to play. Terrence had probably been playing it when he died. I wondered when he'd learned to love jazz, certainly not from DeWayne, the only black man I knew whose taste ran to country music. I felt a sudden kinship with Terrence as Trane's wistful tenor filled the room. At the far wall was a table with a hot plate sitting on it, with a chair beside it. I pulled the chair over to the head of the bed where Terrence had presumably lain and looked around the room.

What had he seen when he drew his last breath? Walls covered with ancient wallpaper of faded blue cornflowers. Two or three toss pillows on the bottom of the bed. Was it a coincidence that the color of the pillows and the cornflowers was the same? Had he been making some half-assed attempt to decorate? The posters on the wall, one from the Cancun Jazz Festival and another from the Studio Museum, looked new. *Had he been into art?* A small bar refrigerator was tucked into a far corner. I opened it, prepared to be grossed out. But it was clean: a couple of apples, a half-quart of milk, a half-bowl of leftover beef stew, a jar of peanut butter, half an apple pie. I sniffed the milk. Fresh, the expiration date a week from now. The cinnamon from the apple pie reminded me I hadn't had lunch. I ran my hand across the back and the tiny space behind the compartment that held the ice tray. Bingo. An envelope taped so tight to the surface it took two hands to dislodge it. I opened it quickly, almost tearing the contents: three crisp hundred-dollar bills. I carefully put it back where I had found it.

"Damn!" I said to nobody in particular. I closed the refrigerator, taking more of an interest now in the rest of the room. I spotted the trash can and examined its contents: miscellaneous papers balled up, a bunch of flowers under the papers—mums, goldenrod—too fresh to throw away. I spread a few sheets of newspaper out on the floor and dumped the contents of the can onto it for closer examination: More papers. The note that had come with the flowers, no name. An empty carton of cold medicine capsules. The carton from the apple pie. About two dozen used tissues.

I put the can back and went over to the bed and unfolded the unmade blanket and linen. More tissues. There was a small cabinet above a sink in the far corner of the room. I went over to it, snapped on the light and opened the cabinet. Nothing much. Six condoms, Trojans, neatly stacked in one corner of the cabinet. Listerine. Nosedrops.

There are things you learn on the beat in five years that always stay with you. A second sense, knowing the scent of something that doesn't smell just right, and I smelled it now. Some lazy cop, tired at the end of the day or late for lunch, had proclaimed that Terrence Curtis had lived and died a junkie, and there was no more to be said about it. But I knew different now. If he'd died of crack, he hadn't been an addict, and I was hot for a minute, angry again at the bullshit so many cops put down when it comes to black folks—the official incompetence, the easy way out.

Junkies don't have shit. They can't afford it. They eat crap. They don't have sex. Their lives are about nothing but junk, and whoever Terrence was, he hadn't been like that when he died. I knew that as surely as I knew my name.

This room, filled with half-dead flowers, half-eaten food, Trane playing in the empty space, condoms stacked like candied mints, told me what I needed to know as surely as if he had been sitting here whispering the secret of his life and death in my ear.

I took out the black and white notebook I always carry with me, and noted the place, date and time. I wrote down the place and condition of everything I'd seen—from the medicine to the apple pie in the refrigerator. Then I took out the Polaroid camera I'd thrown into my bag this morning out of habit and took pictures of everything in the room from every possible angle. Five years in this business had taught me to record everything I do, no matter how long it takes or how much a waste of time it seems. You never know where and how the truth will rear its head and smack you on the butt.

When I'd finished taking pictures, I glanced around the room again to see if I'd missed anything. The glint of a silver picture frame leaning against a pile of books on the floor of the far wall caught my eye, and I recognized it as one I'd taken, nine years ago. It was at Jamal's fifth birthday party. Hakim was seven, wearing the same Electric Company T-shirt as Jamal. Terrence was about thirteen, Gerard a few years younger. It was the same year I left DeWayne, the last time they were all together, one magic moment when they'd all been young enough to believe in birthdays. The sight of it made me want to cry.

4

"**W**hat happened?" Jamal asked the minute I walked through the door after leaving Terrence's. He has always been able to read me like a book, and I knew he could tell something was up.

"Nothing," I said, avoiding his eyes and handing him the suit I'd just picked up from the cleaners.

"You found out something, huh?"

"Get dressed," I ordered, dismissing him with a look I knew he wouldn't challenge. Terrence's death wasn't as easily explained as I'd hoped on Sunday, but I didn't want to burden Jamal yet. He'd find out soon enough if there was anything to my suspicions, but I had some checking to do first. He poked out his mouth, grabbed his suit and headed to his room.

I changed clothes quickly, putting on a brown tweed suit I'd bought on sale last summer and a pair of gold earrings Johnny had given me when I graduated from high school. I wear them as a talisman, a good luck charm, and I reached for them tonight almost without thinking about it. I sprayed on Chloe, what I hoped would be appropriate, and headed out.

"You look good, son," I said to Jamal as he came out of his room. I'm always amazed how much a suit can change a kid. He has my brown eyes and my mother's beautiful lashes, which he hates and says are too long. Those eyes darkened now as he spoke.

"Ma . . . did you find out something . . . ?"

"Didn't I tell you I didn't find anything?" I snapped. Jamal is persistent, just like his mother. But it's annoying as hell when you see the trait you most admire in yourself played back in your kid. He looked hurt, and for a moment I felt bad about snapping at him, but I decided it was a mama's prerogative.

"Look," I said as we headed out the door, "we're not going to have time to eat before the wake. You want to stop by Red Lobster on the way home tonight and . . ."

Jamal turned to confront me, anger flashing in his eyes. "Don't think you're going to buy me off with twenty shrimps at Red Lobster. I'm not a kid anymore, and we can't afford it anyway. I have a right to know what you found out." It was his turn to snap.

"Don't be talking back to me. You have a right to know what I want you to know," I said, daring him to answer. We went out to the garage, both of us silent until we were halfway out of the drive.

"I get sick of you treating me like a kid," Jamal said.

"That's what you are."

"Terrence was my brother," he said, staring out the windshield like there was something to see. "I don't care what you say. He was 'blood,' and you're the one always talking about 'blood.' I don't see how you can't understand. You're always talking about how you felt when Uncle Johnny died. Why can't I feel the same way about Terrence?"

"You didn't know your Uncle Johnny, and you don't know anything about the way he died, and if you'd known him you'd know there was no comparison," I said. I hadn't meant it to sound as nasty as it did, but once it was out I couldn't call it back so I snapped my head up like I meant it.

"You don't know how I feel. You don't know anything!"

"What am I doing sitting here arguing with a fourteen-year-old?" I asked myself aloud.

"It's not fair for you not to tell me, and deep down you know it's not fair," Jamal said, trying to be *my* parent.

"So who do you think you are knowing so much about the way I feel?"

"I know you, Ma, and I know you know something you're not telling me about. And it's not fair. It's not fair!"

"Life's not fair," I said, hoping to finally end the conversation. I glanced at him out of the corner of my eye. He was right about one thing: I really didn't know how he felt about Terrence. And he did have a right. I drove in silence for a few more blocks, then I told him what I suspected.

"It just doesn't look like he died like they say." My voice was gentle. "You know that ad on TV, the one that says 'This is your brain on drugs,' then shows an egg sizzling in a frying pan? It's true. Drugs can kill a person's brain. Junkies don't hide money. And they don't eat part of an apple pie and save the rest for later."

"I knew my brother wasn't on drugs!" Jamal said with conviction. "Do you think somebody killed him?" he asked in the next breath.

"I don't know. I'm going to try to dig up the police report and see why they figured it was a drug overdose. Whoever checked out that scene was sloppy. There were signs all over the place that he didn't overdose if you thought enough to look for them."

"Can't they do some more tests?"

"It's too late now."

"Ma, who would want to kill Terrence?"

I couldn't answer that question any better than he could, so it lingered unanswered as we headed up the stairs into the funeral home where Terrence had been laid out for viewing.

Morgan's Funeral Home was an old, established parlor on Central Avenue in East Orange situated between a gas station and a convenience store that had seen better days. We were greeted by both the smell of decaying day lilies and Old Man Morgan as we entered the foyer. Morgan always wore a sad, hangdog look that immediately put you in the mood to mourn. His manner was so somber it was almost comical. Once, bored out of my mind at the funeral of the ancient, ill-tempered aunt of an acquaintance, I'd tried to imagine Morgan in the throes of passion. I couldn't. But I liked and respected him. He was a man of his word, and when my parents had died within two years of each other, Morgan had held services for them both. In all the years I've known him, I've never seen him smile.

"It's good to see you again despite these sad circumstances," he said solemnly as he gave me a restrained hug. I got a whiff of Old Spice mingled with formaldehyde as he pulled away. Morgan had buried Johnny too. That memory was fresher in my mind than when my parents had died, and as I entered the cool, dark space I shut it out.

Stained-glass windows made the place look like a church, as did the wooden pews upholstered in green velvet. Morgan pointed us toward the front of the room where DeWayne stood beckoning to Jamal.

"Go on and sit with your father and brothers," I whispered. "I'm going to sit here closer to the back. I'll wait outside for you after the service." I gave him a gentle shove and he headed toward his father without a backward glance. DeWayne hugged him and pointed him toward the space next to Hakim, and Jamal squeezed in beside him. DeWayne glanced toward me, and I nodded in his direction. He looked even worse than on Sunday. Morgan pointed me toward the back of the parlor, and I settled down in the last pew, the prime spot to see who was there and watch who came in.

Who would want to kill Terrence? Although I sensed that Terrence had not overdosed, until Jamal had uttered that question the thought that I could be looking for a killer had not really jelled in my mind. If that was the case, there were two things I knew: One, that the murderer, any murderer, is usually somebody tied to the victim by blood or passion; two, he or she would show up again—strolling by the house, driving by the cemetery, standing pious and proper at the funeral or wake. Anybody is capable of murder—if you get angry or jealous or greedy enough. That's the ugly truth. Some are smart about it, some are just plain stupid; but for every one who does his time, there's at least one son of a bitch walking around who played his cards close to the vest and covered all his tracks.

As I sat there in the quiet of Morgan's parlor, I said a prayer asking God for help and to keep an eye on my boy and everybody else's who finds himself in the wrong space at the wrong time. Then I looked around the room.

Terrence's mother, Delores, sat next to DeWayne in the front pew. Her shoulders trembled as she wept. She'd been DeWayne's first wife; he'd married her in 1971 right after coming up north, long before marrying me. Although I'd seen Terrence from time to time, I hadn't seen Delores in years, and those years hadn't been kind to her. She'd been pretty once. A light-skinned woman with reddish-brown hair and freckles dotting her oval face. The kind the old folks used to call a redbone. Tonight she was wearing a black cotton dress that drained her face of color. She'd been a bank teller a couple of years ago, and I'd heard she'd lately been promoted to assistant bank manager. Up until he married me and his last and present wife Carlotta, DeWayne had often been drawn to "respectable," Goody Two-Shoes sisters—the kind who make their own pie crusts and never give their lovers head. Delores fit the bill. But despite her straitlaced appearance, I'd heard she had a cruel streak that could whip out like a razor and cut a man—or boy—to shreds.

Hakim, his hands folded like a choir boy, sat next to Delores. He still grieved for Amina, his mother. She was the only woman DeWayne claimed he really ever loved—probably because she did him the favor of dying before he got bored with her. She'd passed when Hakim had been a baby, and even though he was being raised by Amina's mother, Hakim looked for a mama in every woman DeWayne brought home. I'd been it for a minute. Maybe Delores had been there for him too. Despite what DeWayne said, maybe there had been good in her.

Glancing up from his folded hands to look around the church, Hakim smiled shyly when he caught my eye. He was two years older than Jamal, but seemed and looked younger and more vulnerable. They shared the same piercing eyes that latched on to you and wouldn't let you go, same turn of the nose and strong chin. But Jamal was taller, inheriting his height from both DeWayne and my side of the family, and Hakim had a look of innocence about him, the kind most boys lost around ten.

Gerard, DeWayne's son by his white wife, Emma, sat on the other side of DeWayne. Gerard, a bronze-skinned twenty-year-old, looked more Arab than African. He'd been a pretty kid, with the kind of hair some folks call "good" and like to run their fingers through, but now his face looked sad and pinched. His mama, Emma, sat behind him, resting her hand gently on his shoulder. As if on cue, they both rose suddenly to go to the front of the room where Terrence's open coffin lay. I decided that now would be as good a time as any to go to the front and pay my last respects, but as I stood to go, a touch on my shoulder and an all too familiar voice kept me where I was.

"Why aren't you sitting with the rest of his women?" asked Basil Dupre, the rhythm of his Jamaican accent giving a sensual lilt to his words.

"You know as well as I do that I'm not one of DeWayne's women. What are *you* doing here?" I threw him an annoyed, sidelong glance. I didn't mean it, and he knew it, but I trusted him less and was attracted to him more than any man I had ever known.

"May I sit down?" Ignoring both my question and forthcoming answer, he sat beside me and smiled. No man I knew could look at a woman the way Basil Dupre could, and even in these solemn surroundings, I felt my body responding in ways I wished it wouldn't.

Basil Dupre could hold my eyes to his the way folks say a snake can. His dark brown skin glowed as if it were warmed from within, and he moved with a panther's graceful power, which I knew could strike either gently or cruelly. He had grown up dirt poor in the slums outside Kingston, Jamaica, and had never forgotten the lessons poverty taught him. There was a hardness about him, a distant coldness in his eyes that never left, not when he smiled, frowned or charmed.

"And when will you keep the promise we made?" he said with a chuckle and a gleam in his eye that told me he knew I hadn't forgotten, even though this "promise" had been unspoken. His glance told me that he knew I was still attracted to him now—as much as I had always been. He was right. I had long ago decided that I had known Basil in some other lifetime before morality and better judgment had a say in the way I conduct my life. Our attraction has always been a mix of desire and wariness that has no rhyme or reason—pure, simple animal lust.

When I'd first met him, I'd been married to DeWayne, and two months pregnant—not showing yet but sick every morning and jubilant about my baby to be and the husband I didn't know. Basil came to the house one night to drop something off. I opened the door and the feeling between us was so electric it moved everything that came into a hair's breadth of either of us—for a minute and a half there was no one else in the room. You read about that kind of thing in magazines, and if it hadn't happened to me, I'd be the last person to say there was any truth to those kinds of attractions, but I'm a living witness. Lust at first sight. I'd never felt it with any man—not even DeWayne—and it scared the hell out of me. I kept my eyes to the floor, not daring to look into his eyes. He was bolder, finding an excuse to touch me.

"A kiss for the new bride," he had announced, and ignoring DeWayne's angry gesture of refusal, he'd swept me up and kissed me with so much passion, I *still* get hot thinking about it. Needless to say, DeWayne was pissed as hell. It may have been the root of his later falling out with DeWayne, but I suspected there was other stuff—the kind men kill for and don't share with women. Presently DeWayne and Basil were enemies.

I felt that Basil was treacherous, the kind of man who could kill somebody and never look back. Yet every time I saw him, my better judgment took a back seat to my hormones, and all I could think about was the way his lips would feel keeping "that promise" on various parts of my anatomy.

But his presence here puzzled me. "Why did you say you came?" I asked again. But before he could answer, Carlotta Lee Curtis, DeWayne's last wife, who I'd heard had just left, grabbed the attention of us both.

5

I had to hand it to the girl, she knew how to enter a funeral parlor. For a moment, everyone who saw her enter forgot they were there to view Terrence. Carlotta Lee Curtis was tall, fashion-model thin, and one of those women who moved like she had always been told she was beautiful. She wore an elegant navy silk suit that fit her like a glove and hit her mid-thigh. She'd thrown a mink swing coat over one arm, and her shoes and purse looked like they cost a week's pay between them. Diamond earrings the size of dimes sparkled from her ears, and her long reddish-brown hair (weave!) bounced down her back like a stallion's mane. As she switched down the aisle toward the front where DeWayne was sitting, the eyes of every man in the gathering were glued to her perfect behind.

At twenty-two, she seemed to know more about the weaknesses of men than most women learn in a lifetime, and she used her knowledge with a power that left you surprised then awed by her gall. I'd heard from Hakim she was jealous of him and DeWayne's other sons—a matter more of money than love I assumed, since he also claimed that she'd tried to sever DeWayne's ties with them. Hakim, who lived on and off with them, had never mistaken *her* for a mother; he regarded her with the respect you reserve for a rabid squirrel.

"That one is a gutter cat," Basil whispered in my ear.

"Your kind of woman," I said.

"You're my kind of woman," he quipped. "But you can't trust that one. I hear she fucks anything in britches, hedging her bets the way alley cats do." I glanced at him in surprise. He gave me his enigmatic smile. Miss Lee, the owner of Terrence's rooming house, strolled in behind Carlotta. She glanced around the place, caught my eye, and then looked right through me with eyes as cold as ice.

"Her aunt," Basil said. "Dead father's sister. Carlotta treats her like shit, but she's the apple of the old woman's eye."

I knew Carlotta's surname was Lee, but I hadn't made the connection.

July, the woman from DeWayne's office, followed Miss Lee. She headed to the front of the church to pay her respects to DeWayne and Delores and then, spotting me, came over and sat down, checking out Basil as she walked down the aisle.

"Samsara?" I asked, catching a whiff of her cologne as she sat down beside me. She nodded with an easy and not entirely appropriate familiarity. She was dressed differently, far more stylishly than before—a charcoal gray dress made fly by a long gray checked silk scarf that she'd tied with a flair. If I'd looked only at her clothes, I wouldn't have known she was the same person.

"Yeah, it's Samsara," she said. "I treated myself a couple of days ago," she added. "It's the new me. Are you and your son going over to DeWayne's place after the service?"

"No," I said. "We're not going to be able to make it."

"Which son is yours?" she asked. "He's got so many I get them mixed up. But he's got one less now, I guess." Her tactlessness shocked me.

"Excuse me?" I asked, not hiding my feelings.

July winced. "God, I didn't mean it to sound so cold," she said, looking genuinely ashamed. "I always talk before I think, my uncle used to say. . . . You know what, I guess it's because I'm always hearing about them. You know how it is—fathers and their sons. God, there I go again. Excuse me," she said in a small voice, her eyes glancing up at me, begging my forgiveness.

"Don't worry about it. I hadn't realized that DeWayne talked so much about his kids," I said. As far as I knew, his favorite topic of conversation had always been himself.

Morgan went to the front of the room to say a few words about Terrence. The minute he sat down, Miss Lee and Carlotta suddenly started to argue. They spoke in heated whispers that drew the annoyed attention of several mourners around them. Miss Lee rose and left the room in a snit. Carlotta turned to watch her go and then turned back around to face the front with an indifferent shrug.

"I wonder what that was about?" July said more to herself than to me. "They don't make too many bitches like that bitch Carlotta. I know I'm not supposed to be talking about my boss's wife like that . . . but—"

"I thought they had separated?" I interrupted her.

"They had for a while, when she threw Hakim out things were bad, but now he's back with her, like a mangy old dog in heat, he can't get enough of her."

"Damn," I said, surprised again by her lack of discretion. My girl definitely said what was on her mind. But her characterization of DeWayne struck me as amusing.

"You must think I've got no class at all."

"You got to call it like you see it."

"It just makes me mad. She does, I mean. I don't even know what she's doing here at the

52

boy's funeral. She couldn't stand him any more than she can really stand DeWayne, but people will do anything for money."

Basil threw her a sidelong glance.

"What do you mean?" I asked.

"Well . . . nothing," she said, quickly. She tossed me a good-natured, dimpled smile, which I assumed meant she really was sorry about her tactlessness this time.

"I'm going to go up and pay my respects to Delores," I said as I rose to head to the front of the room. "Talk to you later?"

"Sure," she said, and as I left, Basil got up too.

"I have some words to say to his father," he said before I could ask why he was following me.

I wanted to remember Terrence the way I'd known him, not filled with embalming fluid courtesy of Morgan's Funeral Home. And as I made my way to where Delores was sitting, I tried to think of good things I'd heard Jamal say about him: his sense of humor, his generosity when he'd been a kid. Anything but the cocaine and how they were saying he'd died; something to help her cope with her grief.

Delores and DeWayne stood together preparing to leave the pew; as I stepped into the space between the bier that held the coffin and the first pew, I extended my hand. But in the split second it took for Delores to acknowledge my presence and lean forward to take my hand, DeWayne caught sight of Basil standing behind me. Unbridled loathing filled his eyes.

"What the fuck are you doing here?" He spat the words out with anger that distorted his face into a mask of hatred. "Get the fuck away from my son."

I have heard the word "fuck" before, even used it myself more times than many folks consider polite, but the crisp ugliness of the word in this setting horrified even me.

"To you, you filthy son of a bitch. May you and your sons rot in hell, *rot in hell*." Basil snarled the words twice for emphasis and spat at DeWayne and at the coffin. He made his point. There was complete silence for a minute and a half as a collective gasp went through the thirty or forty assorted friends, family and business associates of DeWayne and Delores.

"Blasphemy, blasphemy!" I heard Old Man Morgan shout from the back of the room as he headed up the aisle. But before he could reach the front, all hell broke loose.

DeWayne stepped behind me and in the same moment in a single, well-timed motion grabbed Basil by the lapels, shaking him as hard as he could. I dodged out of the way, sliding between him and the aisle. Pain shot through me as I slammed my knee on a pew.

"Shit! Motherfucker! Motherfucker!" DeWayne screamed at Basil at the top of his voice. Hakim looked around from side to side; resting his gaze finally on the coffin containing his brother's body, he covered his eyes and started to cry. I motioned to Jamal to usher him out of the pew and toward the back of the church. But at that moment Basil left-hooked DeWayne with such force, blood and spit flew from the side of his mouth, sprinkling both boys and Delores with pink, frothy spray. Gerard begin to laugh, a chortle mixed with such contempt it made my skin crawl.

"Stop it! Damn you both, damn you both! Damn you, you low-life, couldn't you wait until your son was buried to let start this kind of shit?" Delores cried, holding herself and rocking back and forth like a little girl hugging an invisible doll. DeWayne glanced her way for a second, and in that moment Basil hit him so hard that DeWayne fell over backward, tearing his shirt and landing heavily on Delores.

"That one's for Bettina. You filthy son of a bitch, for Bettina and every other woman you have soiled!"

His words had a ludicrous, old-fashioned ring to them, but the punch that caught DeWayne midway between his left eye and his chin was definitely in the present and so hard it hurt *me*. DeWayne hit the side of the pew with a thud. The blows fell hot and heavy then, and went on—a mixture of spit, blood, flesh and "fucks"—for the next ten minutes. Morgan, with the dignity and speed of a judge whose courtroom has just caught fire, made his way to the front and pushed the bier holding the coffin back against the wall, fearing, like everybody else witnessing the fiasco, that they'd knock it off, spilling Terrence's last remains onto the floor in an undignified heap.

I scooted past DeWayne and made my way toward Hakim and Jamal. I grabbed Jamal's arm, helping him over the back of another pew and finally into the aisle.

"Why, Ma, *why* are they doing this?" he half cried.

I shook my head in disgust, angry and mystified by the whole mess.

"Negroes!" Old Man Morgan chanted, nodding his head from side to side like a disjointed puppet. "Negroes! Negroes!"

Jamal and Hakim, clearly shaken by what had just happened, moved quickly in front of me toward the back of the parlor and out the front door. As we left the place, I turned back to glance once more at the chaos. Both men, panting and surveying each other like wounded animals, were bloodied, their clothes torn. Delores, still shaking, was being comforted by Old Man Morgan. Gerard, still laughing his unbelievable laugh, was being pulled away by a shaken and embarrassed Emma. Carlotta, leaning against the wall near the bier that held the coffin, stood casually smoking a cigarette, a strange amused smile playing across her bright red lips.

"Do you want to stay with us tonight?" I

whispered to Hakim as soon as we were outside.

"He is a bastard, isn't he? A bastard!" I heard July mutter as we were leaving. I didn't stop to ask her who she was talking about, DeWayne or Basil, and I didn't argue with her.

We didn't talk too much on the drive home, and they both went right to bed. I poured myself a shot of Courvoisier, filled the tub full of warm water with something from The Body Shop that smelled like strawberries, and lay back sipping cognac in the scented mist until I couldn't keep my eyes open. Then I pulled myself into bed, lay there for a minute and called the only person I knew I could call at this time of the night and wouldn't curse me out.

He answered on the first ring.

"Tamara?"

"Who else."

"What's wrong? Everything OK with Jamal?"

"Yeah, he's fine."

"Are you OK?"

"I don't know."

"You want me to come over?"

"No."

"Jake?"

"Yeah?"

"Thanks for always being there."

"Where the hell else am I going to be at one o'clock in the morning?"

"Is Phyllis sleep?"

He paused for a while. "Yeah."

"Some shit is going down with this case I'm working on. I need to run some things by you."

"You going to be in your office tomorrow?"

"Yeah."

"I'll be by, sometime before noon. Good night, Tam."

"Good night, Jake."

Pause. "Go to sleep, Tam."

I hung up, rolled over and closed my eyes, thinking about the fight. Then I started thinking about Jake and quickly decided to put him out of my mind. And then I started wondering about what I'd eat for breakfast, and whether I should call the furnace man to clean the furnace, and if I had enough money to pay the cable TV bill this month. And somewhere in the back of my mind, the name "Bettina" lingered, keeping me from restful sleep.

6

I woke up the next morning with a cold butt and a bad case of nerves. The temperature had dropped during the night, and the house was as cold as a dead witch's titty. I went into the basement, fixed the water level on the furnace and threw on an overcoat, waiting for the house to warm up. It didn't take long. My house, a tiny two-bedroom yellow and green two-story Cape Cod that I inherited from my parents, takes about a minute and half to get as hot as hell when the furnace is going full blast. But it would take more than water in a furnace tube to fix my nerves. Just thinking about the way they'd messed up that boy's wake burned me. My mood didn't improve when I opened the fridge and found that Jamal and Hakim had finished off all the juice, milk and toast then crawled back into bed.

"Damn!" I cursed out loud, fixed myself some black coffee—the Jamaican kind—and drank it fast, pissed off at the world. I pushed the urge for a cigarette out of my mind, showered, wrote a note to Jamal, dressed and headed for the small office I keep on the corner of Main Street and South Harrison in the city of East Orange.

I rent office space from my best friend, Annie, whom I've been tight with since grade school. She and William, her husband for the last ten years, bought the building in an auction six years ago. It's a 1940s sad-sack of a place on one of the city's main drags. All the mail to Hayle Investigative Services, Inc., goes there, as well as all my calls. The street floor of the building is taken up by Jan's Beauty Biscuit, a shop specializing in fast perms, long nails and longer weaves. Don't ask me what biscuits have to do with beauty and why Wyvetta, the owner of the place, named her shop after Jan, her mother, instead of after herself. But I guess it has something to do with the loves of her life: biscuits and her mama. Wyvetta is the only woman I know who can eat biscuits with every meal that crosses her lips—from egg foo young to chitterlings.

Jan's is good for a lot of things though: a laugh now and then and hot gossip. You can always find out what's going on in East Orange from Wyvetta or her loudmouthed, goldtoothed boyfriend, Earl. All kinds of sisters—schoolteachers, church ladies, women of "questionable repute"—drop into the Biscuit for services, and if you sit long enough with your mouth shut, you're liable to find out anything you need to know about anybody.

When the need arises, me and Wyvetta also barter services. Like a couple of months ago, her brother was getting a divorce and needed the goods on this dude who was tipping with his wife, but he was broke. I did a week of surveillance for a free perm, two touch-ups and a couple of manicures thrown in for good measure. Today was Wednesday, Wyvetta's late day, and she wouldn't be in until ten-thirty. I checked our mutual mailbox in the lobby for assorted letters, bills and flyers and headed up the stairs.

There are three floors to the building. Wyvetta and Earl did a nice job of renovating their space a couple of years ago, painting the walls a pale rose, each of the stalls a slightly different shade, and laying down white and pink checked linoleum. But the renovations stopped with Wyvetta. The rest of the building looks like (forgive me, Annie) shit. When you start climbing the stairs, a singular odor, somewhere between boiled cabbage and burnt meatloaf, hits you like a fist. I'm used to the smell now; it tells me I'm "home," but it used to bug the hell out of me. I mentioned it to Annie once, but she caught an attitude so I figured it wasn't worth our friendship. Nowadays I just hold my breath on the way up.

My office is on the second floor, midway be-

tween Chan's Chiropractory and Business Ink,
a "consulting firm," basically a lady about
seventy who helps high school kids write ré-
sumés. My place is a large carpeted room
flanked on either side by windows (neither of
which opens), and my orphan aloe plant sits
on the sill of the one on the right. I found it
outside my door looking all bad and straggly
about a year ago, and when nobody—Wyvetta
or Annie—claimed it, I took it in. It's more
than paid me back. I talk to it on a daily basis.
If my face looks ashy and somebody's coming,
I can break off a leaf and smooth the sap on
like lotion. I pour leftover tea on it when I'm
too lazy to carry the cup to the bathroom to
dump it down the sink. Besides all that, it adds
some color to the place, which otherwise is as
dull as bad gravy.

The room is divided down the middle by
my desk, on which sits my secondhand computer. Three chairs stand around the desk, the
odd one behind, the matched ones in front for
guests. A small file cabinet that locks if you
kick it right and a coat rack I found at a yard
sale two years ago stand against the wall. A
table topped by an electric kettle, two cups, a
box of sugar cubes, instant coffee (for guests,
I hate the crap) and Celestial Seasonings assorted teas sits beside the file cabinet. Under
the table pushed as close together as I can get
them are a small refrigerator and an un-
plugged portable black and white TV, on

which I watch *All My Children* and *Oprah* when I get bored. I share a small dimly lit bathroom down the hall with Chan and the old lady.

When I first got my P.I. license, I worked out of my kitchen, but there are just too many folks in this business whom you'd rather not see sitting around your house, and I got tired of meeting clients in diners. People don't take you seriously when you talk business over a cheeseburger and hits from the Seventies at Dinsey's diner. Annie gave me a good deal, and so I've been here for about three years. Even though it's expensive as hell and half the time I just break even, I love this place. It's where I come to take stock of life, do my serious thinking and remind myself that I really *do* have a job.

I tossed my coat on the rack, noting with disgust that the hole in its lining seemed to have grown overnight. I filled the kettle with water from the Deer Park bottle in the fridge, and called my service, which is expensive but which, like the office, I need for morale. Whenever I hear Karen, the efficient-sounding sister who takes my messages, saying, "Hayle Investigative Services, may I help you?," it reassures me that I've done the right thing.

"Hi, Karen, it's Tamara Hayle. Got anything for me?" I asked as I quickly sorted through my mail.

"Hi, Miss Hayle, how you doing? Well,

someone name Annie called. Do you want me to read back the message like she said it?"

"Go on."

"She said to ask you, and I quote, 'Where is your rusty behind? I been calling you for two days. Is it a man?' She also wanted to know if you'll meet her for dinner sometime between now and the time you both go through the change."

I grinned despite myself. Annie and her silly behind. She knew she wasn't supposed to be leaving no simple message like that on my business service. I scribbled her name on my callback sheet.

"Two more. One from some lady named Ashley, who said she just called to say hello, and said her son, Benjamin, is graduating from his drug rehab course, and she invited you to attend."

"Benjamin?" I mulled it over for a moment then remembered who he was—a short blond kid, drunk and drugged out, I'd found wandering around Asbury Park the summer before. I guess he'd gotten himself together. "Give me her number. Anybody else?"

"Yeah. Basil Dupre. I love the sound of that man's voice, Miss Hayle. I know I'm not supposed to be saying nothing like that, but I love the way that man talks! Oooh, Lord!"

"Get hold of yourself, girl. What did he say?"

"Well, he asked you to meet him at the

Crystal Lounge on Central Avenue at two o'clock on Friday. Said he heard you were looking into Terrence Curtis's death and had some information about him and Gerard you needed to know."

My heart skipped a beat, and I stopped shuffling papers.

"That was it?"

"That's what the man said."

"Thanks, Karen," I said, and hung up.

Basil Dupre. The hatred that had flashed in his eyes when he'd hit DeWayne last night had come from the bottom of his soul. I wondered why it was there, what he really knew about Terrence's death and his brother, and how much of it he would tell and how he knew I wanted to know. As far as I knew, I was the only person who suspected that Terrence's death had probably not been from an overdose, but Basil always seemed to know more about things than anybody else. He always had a side game, a hidden agenda. I wondered what it was this time.

I settled back into the chair and returned Annie's call. The phone rang about three times before her machine came on. "Pick up the phone, heifer, I know you're there," I said. I heard her chuckle in the background, and then she came on the line.

"Hey, girl, what's up?" she asked.

I grinned. Just hearing her voice lifted my spirits.

"I just wanted to get back to you before we go through the change," I said, quoting her. She laughed good-naturedly.

"I heard about Terrence, how's my son taking it?" she asked, her voice suddenly serious. Annie, who didn't have any kids, had unofficially adopted Jamal, which usually translated into homemade chicken soup when he was sick and extravagantly expensive Christmas and birthday presents. She'd been there for me and Jamal as long as I could remember, through the bad times and the good. "Is he okay?" she asked anxiously.

"As well as can be expected," I said, "but his daddy is going crazy."

"His daddy has *been* crazy. What are you doing talking to that man anyway?"

"Don't make me go into it," I said.

"Tamara," Annie said, with a warning note in her voice. "What's going on?"

"Nothing I can't handle," I said quickly. I didn't feel like a lecture, which I knew Annie would give quicker than a hussy will shake her hips.

"You're not getting involved with DeWayne, are you? Now, Tamara, you know . . ."

"No, of course not," I said quickly. "Give me some credit, Annie," I added, slightly annoyed.

"What then?" Annie asked, not letting me get away with saying nothing.

"You remember Basil Dupre?" I finally said,

throwing her a bone. I knew she wouldn't be satisfied until I told her something.

"Basil Dupre!" She screamed into the phone like a teenager. "No woman who still has hormones could forget that Basil Dupre!"

I paused for a moment. "He called me."

"Called you? Go on, girl. Did you all ever . . . ?"

"No."

"You know what I've got to say about that, Tamara, don't you? Girl, you've got more control than my Aunt Betty."

"Aunt Betty!" I screamed. Annie's Aunt Betty, a proud and vocal virgin all of her life, had been the butt of our jokes ever since we'd reached puberty.

We both laughed at the thought. "I'm not as bad as Aunt Betty."

"It's good to be careful, but not *too* careful," Annie warned. Annie, happily married to her first love for most of her adult life, loved to offer advice and encouragement about my nonexistent sex life. I took it with a grain of salt. She had *no* idea how bad things were out here.

"Why did he call you?"

"Business."

"Risky business. Have you ever known a brother as fine as Basil who wasn't trouble? He definitely does have that dangerous edge."

"Yes, that he does. Can we not go into it

though?" I said, not wanting to talk about Basil either.

"Girl, what's wrong with you?" Annie snapped.

"Nothing, I've just got a lot on my mind," I said.

"You sure you're all right?"

"Fine, Grandma," I said, calling her the nickname I sometimes called her when she worried about me.

"But I really do have to to go," I said after a minute. I knew how a five-minute conversation between us could quickly turn into half an hour. "I just called to see what was up. Do you want to get together next Sunday at The Priory?"

"No, that won't work for me. That deal William's been working on in Ghana came through, so we're going to Accra for a couple of weeks. We're leaving Friday morning."

"Accra! I don't believe you, Annie! You better bring me back some kente cloth."

"I will. In fact, that's really why I called. I just wanted to touch base with you before we left. Give the baby a kiss for me?"

"Baby? I know you're not talking about that big-mouthed fourteen-year-old who lives in my house," I said with a chuckle. "Give William a hug, and you all have a good time in the Motherland."

"Okay, girl . . . Basil Dupre, huh?"

"Bye, Annie!" I said with mock irritation.

"Bye, sweetie. Take care of yourself."

The kettle went off, and I poured hot water over two Lemon Mist tea bags and settled back in my chair, turning Basil and his message over in my mind. I could hear Wyvetta and Earl opening up the Biscuit downstairs and figured it must be close to ten-thirty. I turned on my computer, took out a new disk and created a file: DeWayne Curtis, naming it CD5 (Curtis DeWayne Five, for the number of his wives). I typed in the date on the top of the screen, and the rate I'd be charging DeWayne per day. Then I typed in the name of everyone whom I'd seen over the last twenty-four hours who was even remotely connected to Terrence: Carlotta, Gerard, Basil, Hakim, Miss Lee, July, DeWayne, Delores, Emma, Old Man Morgan.

I took out the notebook in which I'd recorded my observations at Terrence's apartment and typed in all the things I'd found—from the nearly dead flowers, to the empty carton of cold-medicine capsules to the three hundred-dollar bills and the food in the refrigerator.

My notes are free-form—words, phrases, impressions that don't make sense to anybody but me. If a computer-literate crook should ever break into my office, figure out how to get into my computer and actually manage to call up a file, he'd have *no* idea what the hell I was writing about. But my notes are important to me. They help me keep track of my progress on a case on a daily basis, and it's amazing how firsthand impressions can take on new meaning when you look at them in the company of firm data. You never know what's important until you start putting things together.

Carlotta's smile. I'm not sure why I typed it, but there it stood in pea-green letters on my black screen. That inappropriate, amused flash of red had struck me strange then, as strange as Gerard's leer.

I wondered if Wyvetta had anything on Carlotta. *Somebody* had to do that weave, and although I'd never seen her downstairs, Wyvetta is the best in the business. You can learn a lot about a woman in the time it takes to do a weave. I made a mental note to drop into the Biscuit for a manicure. *Wyvetta.* I typed her name in just so I wouldn't forget to talk to her, chuckling as I did it. Old Wyvetta would be pissed as hell if she knew I was typing her name into a computer file on a murder case. *Murder*, that word came up fast. It *could* have been an accident. There had to be a motive for murder. *Who would want to kill Terrence?* Jamal's question popped up as quick as if he'd been sitting here. Jumping to conclusions? Maybe. But there it stood, typed out like "Carlotta's smile." *Let it roll?* I thought to myself. *Let my inner mind to its work*, as Annie would say.

"I'm getting silly with this mess now," I said out loud. "Silly, just plain simple!"

"Yeah, simple for not keeping your door locked. What the hell kind of ex-cop are you?" said Jake as he entered my office, taking me completely by surprise.

"I thought I locked it."

"Look again." He jingled the doorknob to demonstrate, and the lock shook obediently. "You think somebody might have tried to jack it open?"

"I'm not into anything that heavy yet. I just started."

"Got a screwdriver?"

I looked in my drawer, reached around to the back and found one wedged between an old issue of *Essence*, an empty box of Junior Mints and a half-filled box of tampons and tossed it to him without really looking. He caught it with one hand like a pro before it could hit him.

"Lethal weapon in the wrong hands. A few inches lower . . ."

"Sorry, I didn't mean to aim that low, not with a screwdriver anyway."

"You're making me blush, Tam."

"Nothing makes you blush, Jake."

He cackled mischievously and began working on the lock on the floor.

I always forget how fine Jake is. Usually it's the reactions of other women that remind me, those whose eyes watch him stroll into a restaurant or walk across a hall, that little breath that receptionists, nurses, librarians take when he asks them a question. The riveted attention of the women in a jury when he stands up to give his opening statement. His skin is smooth and dark chocolate brown. I used to tease him, telling him it was as soft and pretty as a girl's, but there's nothing girlish about him. He has one of those chiseled Ashanti god faces, the kind you know would have belonged to a king in the old days—Michael Jordan fine. He's tall, definitely built, but not overdone. Strong, but his power is spiritual as much as physical, something you sense about him, the kind other men instinctively respect and that women intuitively want to blend their bodies into. He's the kind of man who would give his last dime to somebody who needs it, but is definitely not afraid to throw down with everything he's got anytime or anyplace if the situation calls for it. He's a few years younger than Johnny, and when I was seventeen and saw him the first time I *knew* I was in love.

But I had no idea then the roads our relationship would take. He's been different things to me in different times of my life, and our feelings go deeper than lust or even love. He followed Johnny into the Department, but left bitter and angry and went to law school to become a Public Defender—protecting people from a system he knew was stacked against them. But he isn't a crusader; he does what he has to do and never talks about it. I call him more than I should—when I can't make sense of a case or I just need to run something by somebody or I just need a shoulder to cry on. His instincts for this business are the best I've ever seen. It scares me to think that he's probably the only man that I could ever really love.

He finished fooling around with the door and sat down on the chair beside me. I caught a whiff of his cologne mingled with his natural scent.

"So what won't let you get a good night's sleep?" he asked, leaning back in his chair.

"Want some tea?" Even though I'd called him, suddenly I wasn't eager to tell him about this mess with DeWayne. But he knew my tricks.

"That bad?"

"I just asked if you wanted some tea."

He grinned. "None of that herbal mess you keep around here."

"Instant coffee?"

"OK." I plugged the kettle back in and put some granules in a cup.

"That asshole you were married to is fucking you around again, huh?"

I looked at him in surprise and then we both laughed. "What's he up to this time? 'Fess up."

"I'm doing some some work for him."

"Work? Jesus, Tamara!" A look of disbelief

spread across his face as he shook his head in disgust. "What is wrong with you? Why are you letting that fool back into your life? Is it the money? You know you can come to me if you need some money!" He spoke fast and furious—the words following each other rat-a-tat-tat like a machine burst. He stopped long enough to put his cup down, shake his head and roll his eyes for emphasis. The kettle went off, and I poured the water into his cup, glad to have something to do to get away from his tirade, and sat back down at my desk.

"I felt sorry for him."

"Feel sorry for those who deserve it."

"Did you hear about his son?"

"Which one? The freak or the head?"

"The drug addict. Which one's the freak?" I asked it even though I knew it had to be Gerard. It wasn't Jamal or Hakim, I could vouch for that. "Jake, is Gerard into some kind of weird shit?"

"What happened to Terrence?" he asked, ignoring me.

"They say—the cops say—he died of an overdose, but I'm beginning to think it was something else. DeWayne thinks somebody killed him, and he hired me to find out."

"There are about half a dozen folks—men and women—in this town who would want to see DeWayne dead. But I can't see somebody killing Terrence to get back at DeWayne—although it happens. Terrence was just an addict, maybe sold shit a couple of times, but basically a user."

"Actually, Terrence is the second boy to die. DeWayne's oldest son, who I didn't even know he had, was murdered in a robbery down in Virginia about a year ago."

"Jesus, to lose two kids like that! Even that bastard doesn't deserve it." Jake's a sucker for kids. He has one daughter, Denise, who is a few years younger than Jamal. He took a sip of coffee. "So how's he doing?"

"He was all tore up on Sunday when he came by. He really thinks that somebody is killing his kids, don't ask me why, and he wants me to find out."

"I know he's an asshole, but isn't it kind of unethical for you to take his money for nothing?"

"I'm doing it because I said that I would, but . . . now that I'm into it, there's something about Terrence's death that bothers me, Jake. I don't think there's a plot, but I don't think he died like they say."

Jake took a sip of coffee and studied my face as if he was looking for something I was trying to hide.

"Why don't you run it down."

I told him from the beginning, starting with DeWayne's Sunday morning call, lingering on my trip to Terrence's apartment, ending with the fight at the wake.

"You know as well as me how casual cops

are when black kids die. Nobody really gives a shit. They'll call Terrence's death the easiest thing they can call it so they can go on to something else."

"Maybe he was just a clean junkie?"

"There are no 'clean junkies.' There was too much 'normal' in that room, Jake. Food too good, condoms too new, flowers too fresh. Three hundred bucks in crisp, new bills. Ever see or hear of a junkie who could hold on to more than ten bucks for more than ten minutes? And why did you call Gerard a freak?" I asked him quickly so I wouldn't forget.

"Did I say that?"

"You know you did. What's the deal?" Jake has a phenomenal memory, almost photogenic, and people tease him about it all the time. If he knew any information, I was sure he hadn't forgotten it.

"Attorney-client privileged information. Actually, not my privileged information. One of the other guys in the office has had him for a client a couple of times. My ears perked up because I knew it was your ex's kid. Most of the shit is Juvey, so there's no record to pull, but it's been piling up ever since he turned eighteen."

"What kind of shit?"

"Hustling mostly. Small shit. Boosting, now and then. Petty larceny. Nothing big time."

I considered this, wondering if that was

what Basil had to tell me. "How's Jamal taking all this?"

"About as well as can be expected. Hakim stayed over last night."

"Is what's-her-name . . . Cara, Carla—"

"Carlotta?"

"Yeah, is she still with DeWayne?"

"That's what they say."

"Your ex knows how to pick them. With, of course, one exception." He gave me a wink and then looked at his watch. "I've got to get out of here. I've got a meeting with a client at three, and a lot of stuff to take care of. Denise picked out a coat at the mall that I promised I'd pick up for her, and Phyllis has her appointment at noon."

"How's she doing?"

"Phyllis?"

"Yeah."

"The same."

After six years of asking, you'd think I'd know better, but I asked just the same, and saw again the pain in his eyes. Men's eyes always seem to tell the most when they're trying to hide it. I look into Jake's and I see his soul, and Phyllis is there just like me and like Johnny. I know that about him now.

Phyllis, his wife for sixteen years, has been crazy for eight. The doctors say she's a manic depressive, and she's fine as long as she takes her pills, and mostly she does. But sometimes she doesn't.

We were friends once, Phyllis and I, when she married Jake and when Johnny was alive. There are times when I hate Phyllis because I know he'll never leave her. And then I feel like a first-class bitch. But there are times when I love her for fighting her craziness like she has to do, for loving as much as she can. And I know that even if Jake left her, it wouldn't matter.

Jake, standing up to leave, changed the subject.

"Tamara, if you sense there is something to this thing, go for it. But remember this: DeWayne is one of these dudes that evil seeks out like pins to a magnet, so don't get too close or it will stick to you, too. The gods don't like ugly." He winked again and closed the door firmly behind him as he left.

7

"I don't want to get involved in no shit between DeWayne's ex-wives," July said when I called her to get Emma's number and address. Jake had told me to follow my instincts, and they were taking me to Gerard and his mama.

"I won't tell her where I got it," I said. "And there's no shit to get between."

"There's always shit to get between," July muttered more to herself than to me. But she gave it to me anyway. The truth was I didn't know Emma well enough for there to be anything between us. What I'd heard about her from DeWayne had made me feel more sorry for her than anything else. Her daddy, Sanderson Fuller, was one of the richest white men in Essex County, and her marriage to DeWayne nearly killed him. I'd heard that from Wyvetta, who had heard it from one of the daddy's ex-girlfriends. (Emma had come by her preference in the color of her sexual

79

partners naturally.) Talk had it that he'd disinherited her. She supported herself by substitute teaching and the small handouts her mother gave her before she died.

Rich white folks. That was what DeWayne called Emma—richwhitefolks, run all together like it was one word. After a while, it made me sick to hear him say it and became one of the things I pulled out when I needed something else to dislike about him. But the expression came to mind as I pulled up to Emma's house. *Rich white folks.* Not so rich now.

Her house was a sad little number, off a side street in a white part of South Orange Avenue, up on a hill like it was saying something. South Orange Avenue runs through Newark into East Orange (I live on Chestnut Terrace, which is off of it), and up into rich South Orange, where Emma lived. Many of the houses in South Orange are old and grand, and most of the folks who live there are doing OK, by white or black standards, but neglect was the first thing I saw when I walked up to her house; it had despair painted on it like a coat of Benjamin Moore. The lawn had been run into the ground, until now it was more mud than anything else, bushes grew every which way, and the fence had so many pickets missing, it looked snaggletoothed. I'd tried to call before I came, but the phone was out of order. I pushed the bell and the noise echoed to an empty house. I rang it again, pissed off that maybe I'd made the trip for nothing.

"Damn," I muttered to myself and turned to go. But as I stepped off the porch, glass shattered, and then a scream and voices—a woman's and a man's—came bellowing down from inside the house. Being naturally nosy, I drew closer trying to make out phrases and words.

"You damn bitch . . . stay off my case. You got that straight? It's none of your damn business where I put my dick, you got that straight?" I recognized it as Gerard, his voice high and breaking like a kid's. He said something unintelligible, and then Emma—I assumed it was Emma—started shrieking.

"I've told you, I've told you. Why don't you listen? What if he catches you together? Have you thought about that, Gerard? Have you thought about that? You think you're so clever, but it's not a secret! More people know than you think. If I found out, think about the others who must know!" There was the sound of more glass breaking, and then a wail from Emma that tore at my heart.

"I don't give a flying fuck!" Gerald yelled back. "Not about you or him or anybody but her!"

"Damn you," Emma shrieked again. "Damn you!" Something in her voice alarmed me. I rang the bell again for the third time, and then there was silence. I rang it a fourth time, leaning on it now, and finally Emma came to the door, stopping short when she saw me.

She had been pretty back in the day, in that way white America deemed women so. But the Kewpie-doll cuties age badly: pale skin that wrinkles deeply because it can't take the sun; big, round blue eyes that now held back tears; thin longish blond hair without any body. She was in her forties, about the same age as DeWayne, and looked fragile even though she was about my size. She had on chintzy blue overalls that looked two sizes too big. I knew she was wondering if I'd heard the fight. I relieved her curiosity.

"What's going on?" I asked, trying too late to temper my blunt curiosity with concern. There was a slash of red across her cheek. I wasn't sure whether it was rage or whether her son had just smacked the mess out of her. She saw my eyes go to the mark and started to cry, silently at first, and then her whole body shook. "Can I get you something?" I asked, which was a dumb thing to ask, seeing that we were both standing outside on the porch, but I couldn't think of anything else to say. She shook her head no, then put her other hand in a fist in the corner of her mouth like she was trying to keep her sobs inside. Gerard suddenly came flying down the stairs, heading toward the front door; ignoring me, he threw his mother a long, malevolent look.

"Bitch," he spat. "I see who the fuck I want and do what the fuck I want to where the fuck

I want to!" Emma and I stood there in silent amazement.

"Scummy little bastard," I finally muttered under my breath, but when I saw the look in Emma's eyes I was sorry I'd said it. We stood there in the doorway for a few more uncomfortable moments.

"Do you want to go inside?" I finally asked, as if it were my place instead of hers. She nodded and I followed her inside. The room was small and the drawn curtains made it seem even smaller. Two dirty glasses stood on the coffee table in front of the worn, pale green corduroy couch on which we sat.

"I don't know what to do," she finally said. "I just don't know what to do." She looked up as if she were asking *me* for an answer.

"It's hard bringing them up by yourself," I said. It was weak but the best I could come up with. I knew, though, that if any child of *mine* ever uttered words like that to me, he wouldn't have made it to the front door with his face on.

"I've done the best I can," she murmured. "The best I can." She looked at her hands, avoiding my eyes. "Sometimes I wish he were dead." She went pale, and her lip began to tremble. She put her fingers to her lips, trying make them stop, to call back the words. "I didn't mean that," she stuttered through her fingers. "It's just that . . . I can't control him anymore. He doesn't listen to me. Sometimes

I think he hates me. Hates everything I am, everything I represent."

Rich white folks? I asked myself. "What do you represent?" I asked. She shrugged and looked toward another part of the room.

"Everything he hates," she said.

"He doesn't hate you. No kid hates his mama. Everybody fights with her kid every now and then."

"Not like we fight," she said. Girlfriend was right about that, and she knew I knew it. Even the little piece of argument I'd overheard had a rage to it that was scary. I wondered just how violent things got between them. She sighed long and deep, which hinted at things I'm sure she didn't want me to know.

"Why did you come by?" she asked, as if remembering for the first time that I was there.

"DeWayne asked me to look into Terrence's death," I said.

"DeWayne?" She said his name as if she was hearing it for the first time in her life. "Wow! I almost forgot that you were married to him, too."

The "wow" got me, hippie stuff, like "groovy." I'd forgotten that she was a child of the Sixties, like DeWayne.

"Wow," she said again. "Which wife were you?"

"The second one after you," I said quickly, not wanting to dwell on it. We savored our mutual connection in respectful silence for a half a minute, and then she got up and pulled a chair over to a china cabinet in a far corner of the room. She stood on the chair, then up on her toes and pulled a photo album off the top.

"Would you like to see my pictures?" she asked, like a kid. I was too surprised to do anything but give her a puzzled nod.

It was a large ornate photo album, thick and bound in black leather. Her full name was printed on the cover: Sanderson Emma Whitney Fuller, in gold lettering tarnished with age.

"My real name is Sanderson," she said. "I hated it when I was a kid."

"I can understand that. It's a hell of a name for a little girl."

"That's the way he is. My father. Naming everything he owns."

I had no idea where this was taking us—the photo albums, the conversation, sitting on the couch like two childhood buddies. *Was this a way to get out of talking about DeWayne? Terrence's death? Gerard?* I decided to play it by ear; you never know where something will lead.

"My mother used to call me Sandy when I was little, but he always called me Sanderson. When I got to be a teenager, I made them call me Emma, after his mother." She opened the book to a photo of her as a kid on a horse. The Kewpie-doll looks were cute back then.

"Your mother?" I asked about a plump,

soft-looking woman in a flowered print dress.

"No. Bethann, my first nanny," she said. I knew she'd been rich but I hadn't known how rich. There were several more photos, yellow and torn around the edges, taken at her father's Short Hills estate. She looked like a happy kid—carefree and all smiles—playing on her daddy's boat, standing under a parasol in a garden, frolicking in a ruffled two-piece at the shore. The final one was of her in a long white gown flanked by a somber-looking blond kid on one side, and an old man that I recognized as Sanderson Fuller on the other. Fuller had his arms around her, proudly possessive.

"I hated my father." She said it simply, as if she meant it. I picked up the photo and examined it. It had been taken at a debutante ball where everything was white—the walls, the balloons, the streamers, the flowers. How had DeWayne wedged his way into this world?

"So when did DeWayne come into your life?" I asked, breaking into her trip down memory lane.

She looked at me as if she didn't understand for a moment. "I came into his," she said. "I met him at Rutgers in 1973. I was doing poorly at Smith, and I was taking some summer courses there. We became friends. One thing led to another. We got married. We had a kid a year later. He left me." Anger curled around the edges of her words. "My father hated his nigger ass."

I couldn't believe what she'd just said! *Who you calling a nigger, white girl*? I hadn't heard a white person say that word since I'd left the Department and heard it every day. My reaction was pure reflex: I pushed the anger down to that place inside me where I'd always put it when I'd been on the force. Nigger bitch. Nigger whore. Nigger bastard. Nigger son of a bitch. I'd heard it so much it had lost its meaning. Just another word. I tried to empty my face of any emotion, but she sensed it anyway.

"Now I'm a nigger too, you know," she said, as if responding to my unspoken anger.

Maybe that's your problem. Maybe that's why your son is so messed up, I thought, but didn't say. It was her problem not mine. I was just here to learn what I could learn.

"Do you see your parents now?" I asked even though I knew the answer, courtesy of my girl Wyvetta.

"My father cut me off. My mother died. I don't have anyone but Gerard." She said it with no emotion, no hurt, no love, just resignation.

"I'm sorry," I said. I don't know why I said it, except I was. Marrying DeWayne had been the most daring thing she'd done in her life and she had nothing to show for it but a fucked-up son and the worst-looking house on the block. But then again, there were women who had less than that to show.

"Don't be too sorry," she snapped. Rich-whitefolks pride shining through. Then with a slam of the album, she brought things back to the present, fast. "Up until I saw him Tuesday in that box, I hadn't seen much of Terrence Curtis since he was little," she said. "I really didn't know that much about him. I can't help you." She gave me a quick, dismissive nod. I looked at her strangely. Another curve.

"Gerard is probably the one I should talk to," I said cautiously, handing her my card. "Would you ask him to give me a call? Tell him there's something in it for him." I was lying, of course. There was absolutely nothing in it for him.

"He and Terrence did see each other from time to time," she said softly as if remembering it for the first time. "Terrence was over here a couple of weeks ago. But they really weren't friends, if you know what I mean. More like business acquaintances."

"Business acquaintances?"

"Ask Gerard," she said, suddenly mysterious.

"OK," I said. "I will when we talk."

But it was too late for that in the end.

8

I sat on the white leather sofa in Basil Dupre's living room waiting for him to join me. Everything was white—white walls, white shades, white chairs, white pillows, white rug. I didn't know you could buy so many shades of it. I had poured myself a glass of champagne from the Moët bottle that stood in the glass ice bucket on the coffee table, and Peter Tosh was playing on the state-of-the-art sound system. Basil had called me early Friday morning and asked if we could meet at eight at his apartment rather than at two in the Crystal Lounge. Not too reluctantly, I'd agreed. But now that voice inside me that whispers *danger* when I need to hear it most had started murmuring in my ear.

I'd arrived at his apartment building fifteen minutes early and taken the private elevator the doorman pointed out to the top of the building. When it stopped with a jerk at his floor, I got out but stopped short at the sound of voices: Basil's speaking in a rapid-fire mixture of patois and English, and that of another man. I couldn't understand what they were saying; instinct told me I didn't want to know. They didn't notice me at first, so I pulled back against the wall and eased into a shadowy space between the elevator and Basil's apartment.

The other voice, a burly brother sporting a long jheri curl dressed in a well-cut gray suit, suddenly began to beg in a pitiful, mewling way. Basil turned to leave, but then, as if remembering some forgotten insult or hearing something that suddenly pissed him off, grabbed the man by the lapels and shoved him up against the wall so violently his head left a small greasy spot on the pale pink surface. I gasped and Basil turned in my direction.

"How long have you been here?" he asked in a low whisper, his hands dropping to his side.

"Long enough," I said. I felt vaguely nauseated, gratuitous violence does that to my stomach, and the little voice piping danger was steadily whispering.

"Don't leave," he said as if sensing my intention. He stepped back and opened the apartment door for me. "I'll join you in a moment." I hesitated. "*Please* don't," he said again, as if reading my thoughts. "Go in, pour yourself a glass of champagne. I'll come in a moment." I looked doubtful.

The man, glad for a moment of grace, straightened his suit self-consciously, and while watching Basil out of the corner of his eye, gave me a smile, bowing his head slightly in salute as if to reassure me. Basil, turning away from me, said a few words to him in patois. Against my better judgment, I went inside.

I'd stood in the middle of the living room for a moment, struck by the white-on-white, then trying to figure out what to do next. I'd finally gone over to the couch, sunk down into it and poured myself a glass of champagne. Basil came in within the next moment, completely relaxed now, his smile as easy and seductive as always. He'd sat down, poured himself a glass of champagne and we began to speak as if nothing had happened. But I couldn't forget the scene I'd just witnessed, not to mention the scene at the wake.

"Can we get down to business?" I asked quickly, trying to sound, despite the wine and Peter Tosh, as professional as I could. "What did you have to tell me about Gerard and Terrence? Who is Bettina?" The questions tumbled out of my mouth more quickly than I meant them to, like those of an eager high school student confronting a dreaded teacher. I took a long sip of champagne, and he refilled my glass quickly. I wished I'd asked for tea.

"Why do you ask me about Bettina?"

"You went off on DeWayne like nobody's business at Terrence's wake," I said. "Remember 'May you and your sons rot in hell'? Those were strong words to be saying to somebody whose boy just died. I think somebody may have killed Terrence Curtis and I want to find out who it was. Does Bettina have something to do with this?"

"You really think somebody killed him?"

"Yes," I said firmly. He paused for a moment.

"Do you think I killed his son?" He went to the heart of the matter with a mixture of amusement and disbelief that momentarily disarmed me. "You can't be serious."

"Did you?" I threw the question out to see where it would get me. I've seen violence before, but the killer rage in Basil's eyes that day had unnerved me. Did I think that he had killed Terrence? I honestly didn't know.

"You don't know the background of what you saw in the hall, so don't jump to conclusions," he warned, reading my mind.

"What was it about?"

"A labor dispute. It's so hard to get good help these days." He said it with a flippant, self-mocking levity, and I wasn't sure whether to be amused or alarmed. "You don't want to know," he added, suddenly deadly serious, leaving no doubt in my mind that I didn't.

"I'm sorry that you had to see that. I apologize for it."

"I'm glad I saw it."

"Why?"

"It told me things about you I need to know," I said.

He glanced at me strangely. "But you already knew them."

I cleared my throat.

"Why did you all fight like that at Terrence's wake?" I asked.

"Business, between me and DeWayne."

"What business?"

"Ask him."

"Who is Bettina?"

"So we're back to that again. Don't you want to know what I have to tell you about Gerard and Terrence?"

"I want to know about Bettina first." The look of discomfort that flashed in his eyes when her name came up was unmistakable. My instincts told me she was the real story, and I'd be damned if I wasn't going to follow through.

"I don't want to go into it."

"Why did you call me?" We were back where we started.

"Because I want to fuck you."

Despite the fact that he was stating the obvious, the words startled me, angered me. I couldn't remember the last time a man had stated his intentions so crudely, with so little attempt to charm. I wasn't sure whether I should rise, insulted by his choice of language, or stay put and commend him for his truthfulness. I took a long sip of champagne in lieu of a response.

"You know you want the same thing," he said matter-of-factly after a moment.

"I'm not sure if I do."

"I can tell by the way your body moves when you're near me."

"Don't be so presumptuous. You don't know me as well as you think you do," I said primly. "And I don't know you as well as I have to to get involved like that."

"You know me as well as anyone can," he said.

"Not as well as I need to," I said quickly. "First of all, I don't *fuck* men I'm interested in."

He laughed, with a touch of disdain. "Excuse my choice of language," he said. "In the world that I deal with, we say what we mean, sometimes more directly than some *ladies* would wish. I don't have time to think about the way I'm saying something, just what I really mean to say, what I need or want to do. And you deal in that same world, Tamara. You know that as well as I. Words or the way we say them mean little, call it whatever you want. 'Fuck,' 'make love,' it comes down to the same thing."

"I'm not ready for that."

"What would make it right between us? What do you have to know about before we can do the things that we're both here to do?"

"Speak for yourself. I came here to get some answers."

"You've gotten them."

"Why do you speak in puzzles?"

"Why do you think?"

"Did you kill DeWayne's son?" I asked, bringing the conversation back to where I wanted to it, to where I knew I had some control.

"What do you think?"

"Have you ever killed anybody?" The question had nothing to do with Terrence, but I asked it anyway.

"Have you?"

"No."

"You will."

"I asked you first."

"You know the answer to that, why do you ask it?"

"Why do you hate DeWayne so much?"

"Because he owes me a debt that must be repaid with his blood."

"Who is Bettina?"

"Would you like some more wine?"

I accepted the refill, but repeated my question.

"She was my baby sister," he said quietly. "The anniversary of her death was the day of that wake. And she is dead because of De-Wayne Curtis."

A look of sadness, the kind that comes from memories of lost ones remembered, settled in his eyes. I knew the look; I'd felt it often enough myself. We both settled back against the couch for a moment, and then he begin to speak rhythmically without feeling, as if he were reciting a tale from memory.

"I had come here from Kingston without a pot to piss in, to make money to send home. I did things that I won't tell you now, things I am not ashamed of and would do again if I had to. My father was dead a year. Shot in the head for a gambling debt. I am an only son with four sisters. Bettina was the youngest.

"I met DeWayne Curtis in the dealings I had with the Italians. He was a black man and our alliance seemed a good one. He was older than me. Richer. Faster. Smarter. I tried to impress him." He glanced at me to get a quick read of my feelings, then poured himself some wine for reinforcement.

"I would have done anything for him—to please him, make him believe in me. We were friends. Best friends, I thought. Bettina came to the States to join me. She fell for his lies and the money he spent to impress her. She was young. If not a virgin, then she'd been with a man only once, twice. She thought he was her true love, he broke her heart, but we both

96

know how DeWayne Curtis goes through his women."

His women. He'd tossed those words at me at Terrence's wake. I cringed now when I heard them.

"It was with him that she smoked ganja the first time. But she soon went on to stronger medicine. She died a junkie whore before she was twenty-two." He paused for a moment, and then unfastened a gold locket from a long gold chain around his neck. It had always struck me as feminine, though it took on a decidedly masculine look nestled among the hairs on his chest.

"My first gift to her when I began making big money, when she came to the States. She wore it until the day she died. Solid gold, and she sold herself before she would sell it," he said as he handed the necklace to me.

I thought of Johnny and those gold earrings he'd given me at my high school graduation. Good luck charms from my dead big brother. I snapped open Bettina's locket and examined the face of the young girl inside it. I glanced up at Basil. He was an uncommonly handsome man with an undeniable maleness that characterized every motion, from the way he cocked his head to the gleam in his eyes when he chuckled. But seeing him now in the face of his sister put those looks in a different context. There was a sweetness that I'd never noticed. A tenderness in his smile and eyes.

"She looks like you."

"She was my heart. The only thing that was decent about my life, and her death must be repaid in blood."

"The blood of the father, not that of the sons."

"Whatever comes first." He placed the locket back around his neck. I was stunned by his words and the tone in which he said them. Was he talking about my son, too? He must have noticed the question in my eyes because he changed the subject quickly. "Tell me, Tamara," he asked, "how did you get involved with a man like DeWayne Curtis?"

In that moment he'd sensed my weakness and gone for it with his killer's instinct. He'd asked the one question I've asked myself for the past fifteen years, the one that continues to goad my lingering self-doubt. I hesitated a moment, and then gave him the stock answer I give myself: the one that contains some grains of the truth, but not all of it because I don't know it yet.

"Youth more than anything else," I answered. "Youth and grief."

I settled back then, lulled, I guess, by the wine and a sudden intimacy that was puzzling but completely seductive. I told him about Johnny, how he killed himself and how I couldn't understand it, not then nor now. I told him about those first months after his death, and how sadness and fear can make you do things you regret. He listened, seemingly as drawn into my tale as I'd been into his.

"We are more alike than either of us wants to admit," he said after a moment. "And I am as afraid of you as you are of me. That makes us even."

Somehow I didn't question his sincerity.

He turned my face toward his and kissed me shyly at first, a kiss that sought permission to linger gently on my lips, and then parted them with an urgency that startled me then awakened my desire. His lips traveled over my neck and chin in nibbles, as if he were savoring some exotic dessert.

"Wait," I demanded, and sat up, momentarily unsure.

"Why?" he asked.

I hesitated, trying to think of a reason, but my mind was a blank and my body was full of sensations I hadn't allowed myself to feel for more time than I cared to remember.

I've had lovers in the years since De-Wayne—some remembered kindly, some just a tired waste of my good time. But I'd become careful about men, giving myself only to those I knew would cherish the gift I was bestowing. I seemed permanently between men, and most of the time it didn't bother me except when I worried about just how long this condition would last. That "use it or lose it" mess that Annie was always saying rang in my ears more often than not. Now part of me whispered that this was one of those times when I should tuck reason in my back pocket and firmly sit down on it, but another part warned that another nip on my butt was the last thing I needed at this point in my life.

And there was an undercurrent of violence to him that repulsed yet fascinated me, and that worried me. I don't like to think of myself as the kind of woman who is drawn to violent men. Yet I have always been drawn to danger—that part of me that wanted to become a cop, that likes to drive fast, that plays it on the edge. *Laughing at the devil.* That was what Johnny used to call it. *You like to laugh at the devil.* But Johnny had done it too. Flying around the flame, close enough for it to singe him but not lethally. *Who was this man whose body I could so easily imagine coming into mine and what did that say about me?*

"Do you *really* want us to stop?"

"I'm not sure."

"Tamara, what do you want from me?" He spoke with a mock seriousness that made me smile. "You know that I will never hurt you. Your instincts are as good as mine, and I know you know that.

"There are things that I've had to do in this world to survive. Parts of me that I know seem crude and rough to those who don't know me, but I'm a survivor like you, Tamara. Those parts that you are afraid of will never touch you. I swear on the grave of my sister, Bettina. I swear it."

There was certainly a deadly side to Basil Dupre, a side that I knew, that I had seen, which could quickly slice a man who had done him wrong and not think twice about it. But there was this other side to him too, I knew that now. *Or was I deluding myself? I'd certainly done that before.*

"You're still not sure?"

"I don't know why," I said. He kissed me again as if to reassure my doubts, and he knew instinctively those parts of my body that were the most responsive, the back of my neck, the tips of my breasts, the soft skin between my thighs, and he touched them with his lips, his fingers, his tongue in ways that left me wanting more.

The truth was I did want him as much as he wanted me. I had from the first moment I'd laid eyes on him.

I relaxed as he began to undress me, thanking the Lord that by some stroke of good fortune I'd worn lacy underwear that matched, and not my usual cotton panties and old-lady bra from Sears. He took off his shirt and the locket, a dangling gleam of gold, bounced off his hairy, muscular chest. I was more eager for him than I wanted him to know, and there was no way I could conceal it.

"Are you sure you want to do this?" he asked again.

"Yes," I said, certain now.

"Come," he said, gesturing toward his bed-room with a slight motion of his head.

"OK," I said, "just give me a minute." I kissed him lightly on the lips, and then on his broad shoulders that smelt vaguely of sweat, lust and Obsession For Men.

After he'd left, I sat on the couch for a mo-ment, trying to collect my thoughts. I knew from experience how lonely, down and cheap I could feel after the fact when those after-the-fuck phone calls went unanswered, and I sat at home with nothing better to do than watch Arsenio and obsess about whether his an-swering machine had really picked up my message. I'd come here on business—hard, dry, murder business—and was about to make love with the man who could have done the killing. Was I laughing at the devil, like Johnny always said?

But my choice was clear: I could collect my things, sneak out the door and wonder for the rest of my life what it would have felt like to have him inside of me, or I could go into his room.

Devil be damned, I thought to myself. I checked to make sure that the condom I al-ways carried was still tucked behind my driv-er's license in the photo section of my wallet, thanking the powers that be that it wasn't too old. I dug into the bottom of my bag and pulled out a nearly empty bottle of Shalimar, and sprayed a light mist between my breasts and around my knees.

It was then that I heard the familiar, muffled sound of my pager, which I'd shoved earlier under the debris in the bottom of my bag. Guilt swept me as my home number flashed across the tiny screen. *Jamal.* He knew I was out on business and would only beep me if it was an emergency.

I sat down, blouse half-off, skirt unbuttoned, and called my son as quickly as I could on the extension on the floor near the couch.

Jamal answered on the first ring. He was crying, and he didn't try to hide it.

"Ma," he said. "He's dead, Ma! Daddy says he's dead!"

"Who, Jamal!" I screamed into the phone. "Who? Who?"

"Gerard," he sobbed. "Please come home, Mommy, please come home. My brother died last night!" My breath wouldn't come for a moment. Finally it did.

"OK, baby," I said. "I'm on my way now. Stop crying, baby. I'm on my way home."

I was in a daze as I pulled myself together and went to Basil. His bed was large, lush and begged to be made love to in, and his nude muscular body partially covered by charcoal sheets lay across it in lustful expectation.

"I've got to go home," I said numbly, avoiding his eyes. I could still hear Jamal's voice crying in my head, and it had scared the shit out of me. I didn't want to take the time to explain; I couldn't. I left quickly without looking back.

I was halfway home, speeding down South Harrison onto Central Avenue, when I realized that Basil hadn't told me what I'd come to hear. I cursed out loud. But then a thought came to me that made me nearly rear-end the truck in front of me and caused the hair to stand up on the back of my arms: Yesterday was Thursday, and Gerard was dead. There had been just five days between his death and that of his brother.

9

Gerard Curtis was found dead in DeWayne's mother's house in Belvington Heights, a mostly white suburb north of Newark. The neighbor DeWayne paid to keep an eye on the place found him floating in a tub full of water early Friday morning. The cops were calling it an accidental drowning. DeWayne and I knew better.

We sat in the office of Roscoe L. DeLorca, captain of the Belvington Heights police department, listening to the official version of events. I'd been a cop there five years ago, and this was the first time I'd been in the precinct since I'd left. The smell hadn't changed—same stink of dead cigarettes, funky clothes and cheap coffee brewed too fast and too long. DeLorca hadn't changed either. He was a plump man with a ponderous manner and a slower smile that could be charming or sinister depending upon how he started his day. His face seemed to fall into itself so he always looked slightly disappointed, and his narrow gray eyes looked like they always suspected the worst. On a bad day he resembled every caricature of an ugly cop I'd ever seen.

But I liked and respected DeLorca. In the years of my struggle as the lone female, lone black cop on the force, he'd never pitched me a raw deal or been afraid to face down fellow cops—even those he got drunk with Friday nights who preferred to see a "nigger bitch" dead or lying on her back rather than sporting a badge like she deserved to wear it. For five years, DeLorca had been my reluctant mentor and protector, and he'd been pissed when I quit: Mad at me because he'd believed in me and at himself because he didn't like to lose. But I was here this Saturday morning in my professional private investigatory role—as the aide to the parent of a dead child, not as one of his "men"—and he wore his kindly public servant persona as he questioned DeWayne.

"So there's been no one living in the house for more than a year?"

"Not since my mother died a year and a half ago. I bought it for her two years before she passed," DeWayne said. He looked nervous. I knew it was because he didn't like cops. "I keep the place locked up now. I put it on the market a couple months ago. Except for agents showing the house, and the elderly gentleman who checks the place, it's empty."

"Were you aware that your son had several arrests as a minor for drug trafficking?" De-Lorca asked.

De Wayne took a quick, loud sip of coffee.

"Yeah. I knew," he said.

"Your ex-wife, the boy's mother, has told us that he has been a regular abuser of drugs and alcohol since he was in junior high school. The reason I'm bringing all this up now is because we think that drug and alcohol abuse played some role in this tragedy. We think that he visited your home, maybe got high on drugs—barbiturates—and alcohol, took a bath, for whatever reason, passed out in the tub and drowned. The approximate time of death was eleven-fifty P.M." DeLorca paused, waiting for a reaction that didn't come from DeWayne, and then continued. If he had glanced at me he would have gotten what he was looking for.

"There are also signs, Mr. Curtis, that your son had been there before. Maybe was staying there part-time—your ex-wife said something about him spending a lot of time out of the house, and we think he may have been there when he wasn't at home. Did he have a set of keys?"

"No."

"Do you have any idea how he could have gained entry to the house?"

A look I couldn't read—shame? anger? pain?—flashed momentarily in DeWayne's eyes, but then he made it disappear. DeLorca noticed it too, and he watched him more closely after that, his eyes riveted to his every movement.

"No," DeWayne said after a moment, regaining control. "I don't know how he got into that house. But what I do know, Captain, is that my son didn't die accidentally. I have two sons dead in less than a week's time, Captain. My son Terrence died last Saturday. Saturday. There are people out here who'd like to kill me, who'd pay to see me dead, and they are taking out the only ones I love, my sons. Somebody is killing my boys, Captain, and nobody gives a fuck but me."

DeLorca took in the tight, determined set of DeWayne's jaw and the despair in his eyes, and glanced down at his notes. It was impossible to tell whether he was taking DeWayne seriously or if he had decided he was just another crazy Negro wasting his time.

"I don't think it's a coincidence, Captain." I tossed in my two cents' worth, hoping to sway him. "There are some things about Terrence's death, the first boy, that are puzzling. I don't think he died of a drug overdose like the officers over there in Newark assumed. I'm not sure if an autopsy was done." I used my best cop voice to make my point. I didn't think that DeWayne was right about there being a conspiracy against him, but Gerard's death had convinced me that he and Terrence were probably mixed up in something together and it had cost them both their lives. I was as determined now as DeWayne to get to the bottom of it.

"Of course there was an autopsy," DeLorca said. "They always do an autopsy when there's a death like that. They don't just assume he died of drugs without proving it." But despite his response, a slight nearly imperceptible twitch in DeLorca's left eye told me that I had his attention. DeWayne saw the twitch too and threw me a nod of gratitude. I nodded back acknowledging it.

He had come by my place late last night to comfort Jamal, and we'd talked until this morning when we'd left together for the station. I'd told him the things I'd seen in Terrence's apartment on Tuesday, and about my visit with Emma on Wednesday, and asked him what he thought about Basil Dupre. Shame flickered in his eyes at the mention of Basil's name, and then he'd changed the subject to Carlotta and he told me how she'd been his salvation. He'd married her two weeks after DeWayne Jr.'s death, and she'd been the only thing in his life that could make him smile then. Now he knew she was poison, but he couldn't get her out of his system. He admitted that he'd used people all his life, and now he was paying for it with everything he held dear. He swore on his mother's grave that he'd put a bullet through his brain if he thought it would keep his remaining sons alive, but he was afraid it wouldn't do any good. They were the most honest words he'd said to me in years, and I'd be lying if I said they hadn't touched me.

"Mr. Curtis," DeLorca said, bringing my thoughts back to the present. "There's no evidence that your son Gerard was murdered. The coroner has not yet completed his full report, but the evidence indicates that alcohol and drug abuse was going on prior to the drowning. There was a slight bruise on his right ankle, but that was very likely something that he'd gotten before. There is no indication of anything out of the ordinary. We assume he was alone when he died."

"Would it be possible for us to see the report?" I asked. DeLorca threw me a glance out of the corner of his eye that reminded me of the unspoken code of the Department: Share as little as possible with anyone who wants to know.

"Mr. Curtis will be receiving a copy of the death certificate as soon as the autopsy is complete and the certificate has been signed by the medical examiner," he said, leaping from Mr. Public Relations to Mr. Authority.

"You said something about evidence," DeWayne broke in. "What evidence?"

DeLorca shook his head. "There is no hard evidence, but murder by drowning is very rare. This one was accidental."

"But you can't be absolutely sure," I said.

"Nothing's absolutely sure, Hayle. You know that as well as I do." He'd momentarily forgotten my new status and was barking at me like he used to do when I was in the Department. He rang for a police clerk, who quickly appeared, eager to offer assistance.

"Hansen, take Mr. Curtis over to the coroner's office to pick up his son's effects," he said in a low voice. "Ms. Hayle," he said to me, emphasizing the "Ms." "Could you stay for a few more moments?"

As soon as we heard DeWayne and Hansen's footsteps in the distance, DeLorca turned to face me. "What's your involvement with all this?"

"DeWayne is my ex-husband, Jamal's father."

"Oh," he said, recalling, I guess, what he could of my personal history. "How's the boy doing?"

"He's doing good, Chief," I said, slipping into our old familiarity.

"How old is he now?"

"Fourteen. But still big for his age." It was a throwaway line, but DeLorca nodded, shifting his eyes down to his desk, avoiding mine. I knew then that he still remembered.

Jamal had been nine when it happened—the reason I left the force, his initiation into black manhood. I'd asked Marvin Wiggins, the teenager next door, to watch him that night. Mar-

vin was a good kid, football player, popular,
all young black manhood with a silly grin and
a B-boy style that Jamal adored and sometimes
imitated, much to my chagrin. I was working
the six to two and Marvin and some of his
"boys," other teen-agers who lived nearby,
were going to Willowbrook Mall for me to buy
Jamal some sneakers. They headed to the station to pick up the money I'd forgotten to give
them, driving fast since they'd started at eight
when the mall closed at nine, probably faster
than they should have been. They were also a
car full of young black men cruising through
Belvington Heights after dark in a late-model
car, and that meant trouble.

They, my brethren in blue, pulled them over
because of the speed, they said, to a side street
off the road, and got nasty when Marvin gave
them some lip. They bloodied his nose for being
ing a "smart-ass nigger" then knocked him
around for good measure and asked if "anybody else wanted some." Jamal peed his
pants. When he started to cry, they knew he
was a kid, "big for his age," got scared and let
them go. But some cops like to brag.

Five big black bucks. I heard somebody joking
about it in the locker room. I didn't know what
they were talking about until DeLorca called
me in an hour later to tell me what had happened. He'd heard it by then from a not-too-
bright rookie cop they threw off the force six
months later. DeLorca knew the kid was mine

(four big black bucks and one little black buck, my son).

DeLorca, red-faced with rage, assured me that the cops would be punished appropriately, but I could feel my dinner rising in my throat. I just nodded and then went into the nearest can and threw up the chili I'd eaten two hours before.

I won't forget Marvin's mother when I walked in that night. She'd come to stay with Jamal until I got home. I won't forget my son's eyes either. I quit two weeks later, and everybody except Jamal thought I was crazy, but he was the one who counted.

"How are things going otherwise?" DeLorca asked, looking me in the eye now. He was and always had been a man of the now, and he refused to feel guilty. He thought I should have been tougher, but he'd never been a mother. "How's business?"

"Fine," I said. "The usual stuff, insurance scams, lost kids, cheating husbands, murders cops won't touch."

"Jesus Christ, Hayle! This isn't murder. Why are you taking it there?"

"Because it *is* there, Captain," I said. I tried to hide the fear in my voice. I knew if I sounded hysterical DeLorca would dismiss me without a thought, the way cops are prone to do.

He lit a cigarette, ignoring the two dusty NO SMOKING signs on his wall. "Like I just told the boy's daddy, Hayle, drownings are rarely murder, you know that as well as I do."

"And you know as well as I do that there's no definitive test for murder or suicide by drowning. It can go either way. You say it's accidental, but there's no definitive way you can't say it's not murder."

"There was no sign of anybody—man, woman, beast—being in that room when the kid died. No signs of a struggle. We figure he came into the house to do drugs. The kid had a juvey record; he was a known dealer and abuser. For all we know, he might have been selling drugs out of his dead granny's house. Maybe he took a bath because he was getting ready to meet somebody, maybe he was even going on a date, I don't know. If the shower had been working, maybe the kid would still be alive. So he took a bath, drunk, high on cocaine. Fell asleep in the tub and drowned to death—à la Jimi Hendrix."

"Jimi Hendrix choked on his own puke; he didn't drown in a tub, and he had two groupies with him."

DeLorca waved his hand in dismissal. "No murder. Hayle, you're barking up the wrong goddamn tree. Earn your money somewhere else. We know what we're doing here. And it ain't looking for a killer."

He tossed me a set of photos of Gerard taken at the death scene. "Here, Jessica Fletcher," he said. "Check these shots out. You think you can find murder in these, Miss *Murder, She Wrote*? Just a dumb, dead kid drowned in a tub, nothing more."

I glanced down at the stark black and white photos and lost my breath. I remembered Gerard, alive and cursing out his mama on Wednesday afternoon, dead by Thursday night. I hadn't liked him. His *mama* hadn't even liked him, but his pale, naked body looked small and vulnerable floating in the old-fashioned claw-footed tub. I shuffled through the photos taken from different angles, some at the death scene, some close-ups of the body before the autopsy. I felt nauseated; I always do when I look at a corpse.

"When will the medical examiner be finished with his report?" I asked, handing them back to DeLorca.

"Later on this week, and I know what they'll find. Accidental death by drowning."

The door opened and DeWayne, ashen-faced, eyes watery, came back in. In one hand he carried a brown paper bag filled with Gerard's personal effects. In the other he still absentmindedly carried the lousy cup of coffee that he'd had when he left. DeLorca extended his hand to shake. DeWayne put the coffee down and grasped it.

"My condolences, Mr. Curtis," he said. DeWayne nodded weakly in acknowledgment. We thanked DeLorca for his time and headed out. We drove in dead silence through

Belvington Heights back to East Orange, and said nothing to each other when he finally dropped me off.

My house was empty when I walked in. I started thinking about Gerard. Six years ago he'd been just about Jamal's age. I wondered if he had ever been like my son. Teasing his mama, playing basketball, dreaming of nothing more than what he'd do on a Saturday night? When did it start to go wrong? Six years, six days, six hours can change a life. They were the same blood. He and Jamal. Same blood. A chill went through me, past my bones into my soul.

Somebody walking on your grave, my grandma used to say when I was a kid and felt a chill like that. It would scare the hell out of me.

But, Grandma, I'm not dead yet.

Don't need to be dead for somebody to be walking on your grave. Or your son's grave.

I poured myself a shot of brandy even though it was just past noon, hoping I wasn't becoming a lush. When Jamal walked in, I poured it down the sink.

"Where have you been?" I asked him.

"Playing ball."

"Where?"

"At the court."

"You know you're supposed to let me know where you're going. Why didn't you tell me you were going to play some ball? What the hell is wrong with you? You know damn well you're supposed to leave me a note or call or tell me where you're going."

"God, Mom, what are you yelling about for Christ's sake! It's twelve-thirty in the afternoon. I'm not a damn baby!" He threw his hands up in disgust and rolled his eyes. "God, what's wrong with you?"

"Don't curse at me."

"You cursed at me!"

"My nerves are bad."

"Your nerves are always bad."

"I want you to be careful, Jamal," I said.

"Why?" he asked, throwing me a suspicious glance.

Except for his call to me at Basil's and a brief talk when I'd come home, he hadn't mentioned Gerard's death or how close it resembled Terrence's or if there was any connection. He had talked to DeWayne when he'd come over, but he'd kept things tight—man to man, he didn't want to be a baby in front of his daddy. But I knew he was scared. He had to be.

"Come here, Jamal," I said.

"Why?"

"Just come here."

He came over and sat down beside me.

"Are you worried about what's been happening? About what happened to Gerard?"

He paused, thinking hard before he finally answered. "No," he said defiantly. "I ain't scared."

"Don't say 'ain't.' "

"Why are you always on my case?" he screamed at me, and then deciding, I guess, that he owed me something else, let out a sigh that sounded like he was carrying the weight of the world. "I heard you all talking last night, and Dad said something about all these accidents not being accidents. About somebody being out to get him. How he couldn't make it stop."

"There's nothing to stop."

"Is somebody going to try to kill me?"

"No, of course not." I said it too quickly, and he knew it.

"How do you know?"

"I just know. That's all." I answered in the old What-I-say-not-what-I-do tone that always comes in handy, and I knew I had to say more. "Nobody is out to get DeWayne," I said as convincingly as I could. "Terrence and Gerard's deaths may have been connected. Both of them may have been involved in some shit that we don't know about yet. I'm trying to find out what it was." Jamal gave me a slight "caught you" smile when I said "shit." Then his face turned serious again.

"The stupid cops never arrest anybody when they've done anything. How come they don't investigate like they're supposed to? What are you going to do, Ma?"

"I'm doing all that I can. Talk to some more

people . . ." I left it there because I wasn't sure where else to take it.

"Are the cops going to do anything else?"

"They will as soon as there's more proof. But they can't do anything now. Both deaths have been ruled accidents."

The doorbell rang then, and Jamal, assuming it was for him, popped up to answer it.

"Hi there, is your mom home?" a vaguely familiar voice asked. "I'm from your father's office."

"Ma, it's a lady who says she's from Dad's office," he called from the door, and bounded back inside and up the stairs. "Ma, can we talk later? I'm going to meet Hakim over at the court on South Orange Avenue and then we're going back over to Jerome's to play some videos. If Hakim calls, tell him I've left already."

"Yeah," I said. "Be back before dark."

"Before dark!? God, Ma, Jerome lives right over there on Evergreen Terrace! Come on, Mom."

"Be off that court before dark," I said. I could hear him muttering to himself as he ran upstairs and then out the back door.

July, grinning, stood at the door listening to our conversation, holding a large tan envelope in her hand.

"Hi," she said good-naturedly. "I came by to give you this. I was supposed to mail it to you but you're on my way home, and I figured, why waste a stamp? Is that Jamal?" she asked as the back of Jamal's head disappeared out the back door. She was wearing an over-sized Gap sweatshirt and a tight pair of jeans. She looked fresher, younger than she had the other times I'd seen her. She seemed more confident too, and that rural accent she'd had the first time I'd talked to her had vanished completely. I wondered again if there was anything going on between her and DeWayne. They say a man's attention can bring that kind of light to a woman's eyes if she needs it, and I'd felt instinctively that July had needed something.

"Yeah, that's Jamal," I said. "What are you doing working on a Saturday?"

"I usually don't, but with all these tragic happenings, I've been putting in some extra hours."

"What do you do for him, anyway?"

"Type, answer the phone, stuff that needs to be done. I do what I need to do to get by," she said, handing me the envelope. "This came in the mail, it looked official and I called DeWayne about it. He said to put it in an envelope and mail it to you."

"Come on in for a minute," I said as I opened the large envelope, which contained a smaller, official-looking one. It was from the Newark Department of Health and Human Services, and I realized it was a copy of Terrence's death certificate. I put it on a side table to be opened and examined later on.

"God, I envy you," July said, surveying my living room as she walked in. I hadn't cleaned the place since last Sunday when the whole mess had started, and it looked that way. I wondered what the hell she was talking about.

"You envy me?"

"Yeah."

"Why?"

"You've got it all together. You've got your own business."

"Making *no* money."

"A nice house."

"The money pit? Actually, it belonged to my parents. I inherited it."

"You've got a nice kid."

"Motherhood is not all it's cracked up to be, believe me," I said. "You want something to drink? Some tea? Soda?"

"A soda sounds good."

I got us both a Sprite, and we sat down on the couch, sipping in silence.

"DeWayne mentioned he hired you to find out what was going on."

I was surprised that he'd mentioned it to her. Maybe there *was* something going on. "Haven't found out much yet, but something will turn up eventually, it always does." I sounded more confident than I actually was. *Nothing* has to turn up eventually.

"You said at the wake that you wanted to ask me some questions. What did you want to ask me?" She took a sip of soda and crunched a piece of ice.

"You said something about knowing a lot about DeWayne and I just wondered what you meant?" I asked.

"Nothing. Just talking," she said, sucking on the ice, biting it hard. "Just running my mouth. Wasn't that a weird scene at the funeral?"

"Weird isn't the word I'd use," I said. "Just sad. Very sad. Disrespectful."

"Well, at least they had a funeral."

"Have you ever known a dead person who didn't have a funeral?" I asked playfully.

"Yeah, plenty," she said very seriously, taking another sip of soda, her eyes dropping down. "I won't have a funeral."

"Of course you'll have a funeral, July! *Everybody* has a funeral," I said. "Someone will care about you enough to pay your memory its due. Talk about weird, that's a weird thing to say."

"I'm in kind of a weird mood. I had a birthday last week," she said quickly, as if apologizing or changing the subject. "I was thirty on October first. But everybody in my family is dead. So there was nobody to celebrate with me. Nobody to celebrate, nobody to mourn. Nobody but me." She said it with a wistful sadness that hit me in my gut. I liked her despite her quirkiness.

"My parents are dead, too—"

"My mother killed herself," July added quickly before I could finish. She said this almost offhandedly, without sadness, and there was no coming back with anything comforting to say, except the one thing I could share.

"My older brother Johnny killed himself, too," I said after a moment. "He shot himself through the head about sixteen years ago. I'd just turned twenty."

July glanced up at me; a look of kinship—maybe gratitude—in her eyes told me I'd done the right thing. She took my hand, held it gently for a moment and then let it go, as if she'd suddenly turned shy.

"At least your parents, your brother, left you this house," July said. "My mama didn't leave me shit."

It was strange the way she said it, going from Johnny's death to the house like that, but my life had been marked by young grief too. I knew the signs. July had them, and this was one: the inability to let yourself feel. God knows, I'd done it. Sometimes death came down to what was tangible—a dead mother's favorite earrings: the desired object of squabbling, grieving sisters. Anything you could touch so the pain wouldn't touch you. July was right. I did have the house, the spoils of death left by my parents and Johnny. But July had something too.

"You," I said, after a moment. "Your mother left *you*, you—July."

"That's not enough. Do you ever feel that way?" she asked with a sudden intensity.

"Sometimes."

"I read all the self-help books on self-esteem I can. They tell you to find the source of your pain and cut it out. That's what I'm trying to do. Slowly but surely. One cut at a time."

"That's as good a way as any," I said.

Her weird edge made sense now. I had it too at times.

"Let me go home and face the empty-house-Saturday-night-blues," she said with a light-hearted chuckle that told me she wasn't taking herself too seriously, making lemonade from lemons like Pet, my eternally optimistic sister, always tells me to do.

"Want to get together for lunch sometime?" I asked, almost without thinking.

"Sure," she said. "I'd love to." I walked her to her car.

"Happy belated birthday," I said.

"Thanks," she yelled back through the window as she drove away. "Let me know when yours is, maybe we can celebrate."

I went back into the house, a smile still on my face for July. I opened the envelope within the envelope, scanning the contents of the form quickly. Terrence had died from an overdose of cocaine. He *had* been taking drugs. I felt angry and betrayed, which was stupid because *he* was the one who was dead. He couldn't have been murdered. You can't *force* somebody to OD on cocaine. DeLorca was right.

"The wrong goddamn tree," I said aloud, jamming the document back into its envelope. "The wrong goddamn tree."

10

I woke up at five that next morning and lay there listening to the furnace rumble and watching the minutes on my digital clock click from 5:05 to 5:06 to 5:07. When it reached 5:30, I sat up and switched on the light. Half an hour had blinked by, and here I was again, missing another Sunday morning's worth of good sleep. Damn. Five-thirty in the morning used to be cigarette time, and I almost regretted giving them up. But a cigarette was probably the last thing I needed.

Terrence *had* died of a cocaine overdose. And the photograph of Gerard's body floating dead in the claw-footed tub had etched itself into my mind, chilling me every time I thought about it. What was the connection?

I lay back down, not ready to get up yet. I stretched long and slow, feeling the full length of my body and remembering how Basil's lips had felt when they'd touched me Friday night.

Desire for him swept through me as I lay in a sensual netherland between sleep and awake imagining his lips caressing my neck and back, imagining the way he would have felt if I had stayed. *Bettina.* I couldn't get his story of his sister out of my mind.

But then a thought came that smacked me awake like somebody's mama. *Was he telling me the truth? Or had he been trying to throw me off his track?* For all I knew, his whole story could be a crock; Bettina could be alive, well and eating saltfish and ackee back in Kingston. Or maybe she didn't exist. *Why had I never heard about her from anybody else? When had all this taken place? Could I really trust him?* The phrase he'd used to describe Carlotta suddenly came to mind: "fucking anything in britches, hedging her bets the way alley cats do." Was *he* hedging his bets too, fucking "anything in britches"? Was that his game as well?

I have trouble resisting a man who, as the kids say, "smokes my boots," and I'd had a hint of just how smoky them boots would get if I'd stayed with Basil another hour. But now in the cool of the morning, I realized that, yet again, I'd probably let my good sense take a back seat to my hormones.

Basil Dupre. What did I really know about him besides what he had told me? I should know by now that anytime I was attracted to someone there was something wrong with him, and I should run as far as possible in the opposite direction. Annie's words came back to me. "Have you ever known a brother as fine as Basil who wasn't trouble?"

Terrence had died of an overdose, or so the report said, and Gerard had died of drowning. *But it had only been five days.* Five days was too close for coincidence. Possible but close. Basil had access to cocaine. Where had he been when Gerard died? What did he want to tell me that had to be told in the intimacy of his place rather than the public space of the Crystal Lounge?

There was no sense in trying to go back to sleep; this whole mess was starting to work me like an old dog works a shoe. I think best at my office with a cup of Red Zinger within reach. I've never gone to work on a Sunday at six in the morning, and it wasn't something I wanted to get in the habit of doing, but I needed to sift things through again, in my professional space.

I pulled on a pair of jeans and an old T-shirt, scribbled Jamal a note and headed out to the Jetta, which is a diesel and noisy as hell on a quiet Sunday morning. I drove slowly down South Orange Avenue, then down South Harrison to Central, and then made my way to my office on Main Street. The streets were quiet and empty this morning—the saved getting up, the sinners getting home. These days I definitely fit the latter category.

The sun entering my office turned the spiky leaves of the orphan aloe into a tiny monster perched on the window sill. It also gave the room a golden glow; you couldn't see the dust even if you knew where to look for it. I filled my electric kettle with water from the bathroom sink down the hall, plugged it in, and pulled up DeWayne's file on my computer.

WEDNESDAY, OCTOBER 8 came up in bright green letters. I'd made these notes right before Jake came, and that fine, brown body crossed my mind again. I thought about calling him, but it was too early to bother him, I decided, even though I knew he probably wouldn't mind. Jake. Basil. Jake was married. Basil was probably a killer. God, what was wrong with me? I sure knew how to pick them.

I pressed the PRINT button with a vengeance and printed out the file with the notes I'd made last Wednesday. Then I typed a new entry, SUNDAY, OCTOBER 12, and added the new facts I'd learned: Gerard's death on Thursday night, the police version of what had happened.

I looked back at the October 8 list. Terrence *had* died of an overdose, perhaps the most important thing I'd learned this week. He must have been doing dope all along, bullshitting everybody who cared about him. Bullshitting *me* in death. Damn.

But the list still looked odd. Junkies don't

leave half a bowl of beef stew and a half-eaten apple pie. Junkies don't leave three hundred bucks in hard bills taped in a refrigerator. Beef stew. Apple pie. Fresh milk. Ducats.

I pulled out the Polaroids I'd taken of the stuff from his wastebasket: Flowers, goldenrod. They made me think about Jamal and how he couldn't get within six feet of flowers like that without sneezing his head off. My sister had sent me a bouquet of autumn flowers once when he'd been a kid, and his allergies had come down on him so hard I'd had to take him to the doctor for a shot.

It's always the obvious that doesn't belong. Look for the obvious. DeLorca used to tell me that when he still believed I would stick around long enough to make detective. The kettle went off, startling me, and I rummaged through my desk for a box of Celestial Seasonings, plopped a tea bag into a cup and splashed in boiling water.

Look for a pattern. Where was it? There had to be one. Terrence had died of an overdose. Gerard had died in the tub. Two freak, fatal accidents. I don't think so.

Maybe that was the pattern. Two murders that looked like accidents. By someone who knew enough about each boy to arrange and get away with it. But how do you make a twenty-two-year-old kid take enough dope to kill himself? How do you drown a twenty-year-old boy in a tub? Who could hate De-

Wayne that much? By blood or passion?

I glanced at the list of folks connected to Terrence that I'd made on Wednesday, deleting Gerard's name: Carlotta, Basil, Hakim, Miss Lee, July, DeWayne, Delores, Emma. No bells went off. There had to be a motive. Motive and opportunity. And except for Basil, who was obvious as hell about his—revenge— none of them had one as far as I knew now.

More like business acquaintances. Emma's words came back to me. Terrence was a user. Gerard had been a seller. Could that be the connection? Maybe it had nothing to do with DeWayne. Maybe the first death had been a freakish coincidence.

If it was murder, then there had been a method to it, and if there was a method, then I could find it. *The secret of a victim's death is in his life.* Who said that? DeLorca? Jake? It made sense. Terrence lived a junkie and died like one. So what else was new?

I studied the photos again. Flowers. Goldenrod. Autumn flowers, autumn death. Strange when you thought about it. They didn't belong here. Girlfriends usually sent something more obvious, red roses maybe. Who the hell would send a kid like Terrence flowers? Why would he throw them away still fresh? Even in the photo I could tell they were.

Flowers. Kleenex. Empty cold medicine package. Now *that* was a pattern. Smell the flowers. Sneeze your butt off. Blow your nose.

132

Pop a pill. If you're Jamal. Or maybe Terrence.

Allergies run in families. DeWayne had them. Jamal had them. Possibly Terrence had them too. I'd always assumed he'd inherited his allergies from DeWayne's family. My side was fairly healthy. But goldenrod doesn't kill you, and there was cocaine in his blood. So I was back to square one. I looked at the list again.

In his apartment he'd had legal drugs—cold capsules. But capsules can't kill you. Unless they're filled with cyanide, like in all detective novels from the thirties.

So that left cocaine.

I have a couple of textbooks on poisons, guns and other grim topics saved from my days in the Academy that I'd tucked into the bottom of my bookshelf. I picked up one now and searched quickly for a section on cocaine.

Cocaine. Methyl-benzoyl-ecgonine. As I scanned the list, I realized that people didn't just sniff and inject the stuff, sometimes they ingested it. Ingestion was the least toxic means, but poisoning happened. That put everything in a new light. It's much easier to make a junkie suddenly gone good swallow cocaine than it was to force him to start smoking crack again. According to the book it would take at least a teaspoon of pure cocaine to kill a guy of Terrence's weight and height. Or less if something else was added. They don't test for poisons when an autopsy is done unless a specific test is requested. If poison *and* cocaine were used, the cocaine would be picked up but not the poison, especially if it were something exotic that didn't give physical signs after death—like cyanide or strychnine might. I'd bet my parents' house that they hadn't tested for poisons—even the predictable ones. Why waste money on a junkie?

How could it have happened? My imagination went wild.

Somebody knowing about the allergy could have tampered with the capsules, filled them tight with coke and then with something else. Junkies tend to overdose on medications—anything they can shoot, snort or swallow. Get rid of the pain, or itching or sneezing, as soon as they can. Don't wait. Everything is now with junkies, which is why they're junkies. A junkie will take four pills when two will do the job. A bottle of wine when a glass will give a buzz. Terrence, an ex-junkie, had taken three or four capsules in the space of six hours, killing discomfort like junkies do, and if they were filled with something other than cold medicine, they could kill him fast. It seemed farfetched, but at this hour in the morning anything seemed possible.

My tea was cold when I picked it up, and I was too lazy to take it to the bathroom and pour it down the sink, so I poured it on the orphan aloe; Red Zinger was probably good for it anyway. Maybe I was on to something, and I didn't want to lose my chain of thought.

Whoever sent the flowers probably did the killing. I would have to call every florist within a ten- or fifteen-mile radius. There had to be a record somewhere, a bill, an order form.

But did the person who killed Terrence also kill Gerard? There had to be more to it. I reached for the phone to call Jake's number, and then put it back down. It wasn't quite nine, too early to call anybody on a Sunday morning. I wondered if Jamal was up yet. A sudden sense of dread swept through me so quick it turned me cold.

Had I put the double-lock on the door when I left? Had I checked the windows?

I was being paranoid and I knew it, but it didn't matter. The phone rang. I picked it up before the first ring was completed.

"Ma, how come you left so early?"

"I had some stuff to do."

"How come you're doing it on Sunday?"

"I woke up and couldn't go back to sleep."

"Is it something to do with Gerard?"

"No," I lied.

"When you coming home?" It was the first time in two years that he's asked me that. He was usually happy as hell to get me out of the house.

"In a couple of minutes," I said. I'd call Jake from home. "Jamal, I love you."

"I love you, too, Ma," he said, after a moment, surprised by my sudden display of affection. "Will you stop and pick up some Dunkin' Donuts and Egg McMuffins?" he asked, figuring he'd play my mood for all it was worth.

"Egg McMuffins are no good when they're cold."

"I'll nuke them."

"OK. Is the door double-locked?"

"Yeah, I checked it when I got up." A first time for that too.

"See you, baby."

"OK," he said. But I could still hear the anxiety in his voice.

11

Gerard and Terrence were still on my mind as I drove down Main Street, took a turn down South Harrison and headed toward South Orange Avenue. As I rounded the corner to Chestnut Terrace I nearly hit a red late-model car pulling away from the curb.

"Damn," I said, turning into my driveway. I hadn't seen the driver, but whoever it was was moving as fast as me.

Jamal was sitting at the table waiting for his breakfast when I walked in. He was eager to hit the street and play some ball with Hakim in the park, and when I handed him his Egg McMuffins, he made quick work of them, gobbling them down like nobody's business. Any anxiety I thought I'd heard in his voice earlier seemed to have disappeared. After he left, I took a shower, poured myself a glass of juice and started going through the phone book counting florists.

When the doorbell rang twice, a short ring and then a long, demanding one, I took my time answering, figuring Jamal had forgotten his key or had come back to hit me for some money. When I opened the door, Basil Dupre stood on the porch, nonchalantly leaning against my rail.

"How did you know where I live?" I asked, surprised. I was slightly uncomfortable that he'd found me, even though I'd been ready to hop into bed with him two days ago.

"No 'Hello, Basil, I'm happy to see you'? 'Come in and let's talk'?" He cocked his head and smiled. "Hello, Tamara. How are you this morning?"

"Hello, Basil, how did you know my address?"

"You're not hard to find if you know where to look." He paused for a moment, surveying the block. "I was worried about you."

"Worried about me? I can take care of myself. Why didn't you call first? You have my number at my office."

"Today is Sunday, have you forgotten? I tried to get you yesterday, but you weren't in."

"You should have left a message with my service. Why are you here?" I asked it bluntly, realizing as I spoke that my attitude, and I definitely had an attitude, was tied to the talk I'd had with myself (my fear about having been played big time for a horny fool) at five o'clock this morning. But Basil hadn't been part of the conversation. Puzzled, he scrutinized me for a minute and a half.

"I owe you some information," he finally said seriously.

"No labor problems today?" I goaded him, wanting to let him know that I hadn't forgotten the head of that jheri-curled brother hitting the wall.

Basil was visibly annoyed, but he spoke to me patiently, as if he were an indulgent parent talking to a slow child. "Let it go, baby. You don't know what came before it. You don't know what it was about. I'm here because I told you that I had some information to give you, and I wanted you to know that I'm a man of my word."

"And your fists."

"Yeah, and my fists."

The tone of his voice said "Accept or forget me." I knew no more what to make of him now than I had last Friday, or at Terrence's wake, or that first time all those years ago when he'd given me that kiss I couldn't forget.

"OK," I said, after a moment. "Come in, but just for a couple of minutes. My son and his buddies will be coming back shortly, and I don't like them seeing strange men coming in and out of the house."

"Strange men?" A hurt look that he quickly made disappear flashed in his eyes. "In case you've forgotten, I knew you before your son did. And I'll be long gone before he and his boys get back. You really don't trust me, do you?" he asked after a minute, smiling his charming smile.

"No."

"You don't *think* you trust me, Tamara. But you really do. You're a smart woman. If you really didn't trust me, how do you explain Friday? Do you want to talk on the porch?" he added quickly.

The folks on my block believe in minding other people's business and I didn't want mine making the rounds. I stood back so he could enter.

"Thank you," he said with an exaggerated formality, which I didn't appreciate.

He wore lightweight beige wool pants cut to fit, an elegant dark brown cashmere sweater and a black leather jacket so soft it fell like silk. I took a quick glance at myself in the hall mirror as we passed it and didn't like what I saw. But at least I was clean. The fragrance of the dewberry soap from The Body Shop that I'd showered with earlier still lingered on my skin.

"Want some coffee?" I asked.

"Sure you don't mind making it?"

"Didn't I just say 'Come in, Basil, and have some coffee'? You're starting to get on my nerves with your mess."

He laughed a deep, good-natured laugh that made me smile. "Coffee sounds good."

I led the way into the kitchen. "I've got some Blue Mountain I got in Negril when I was there."

"When did you go?" he asked with undisguised interest.

"Jamaica? A couple of weeks ago." It seemed like a lifetime ago now, since this whole mess started.

He sat down at the kitchen table and looked around the room, taking in its distinctive qualities: the grease spots on the ceiling from frying chicken; the burnt spot on the yellow counter where Jamal had put a pan of burning peas; the Popsicle-stick napkin holder Hakim had made me for a Christmas present one year. He looked around and smiled.

"Nice room," he said.

"Thanks." I wondered if he could sense the ghosts—Johnny, my parents—that haunted it.

"This is where you grew up?"

"Yeah."

"It tells me things about *you* I need to know," he said, quoting what I'd said to him at his place on Friday. I measured coffee into the pot and put it on the burner. "What did you have to tell me that you never got around to?" I asked, changing the subject.

"So when will we take up where we left off?"

"After you tell me what you promised to tell me."

"Tamara, why do we always end up back

where we started?" he asked with a chuckle. Maybe it was the kitchen and the perking coffee, or the afternoon sun easing into the kitchen window in a golden, romantic glow, but there seemed to an ease between us now that hadn't been there before, and I joined him in his laughter. Was I imagining this, too?

The coffee finished perking, and I took out two large cups from my pantry, conscious of his eyes on my body, and liking the way it felt. I brought him his cup and then brought out some milk.

"Black," he said.

I splashed some milk into mine and sat down across from him.

"Why did you leave me so mysteriously last Friday?" he asked.

"DeWayne's son Gerard was killed late Thursday. I had to go home to be with my boy," I said, getting to the point quickly and studying his face for a reaction. There wasn't any.

"Gerard Curtis dead? It doesn't surprise me," he said after a minute. "How did he die?"

"He drowned in a tub."

"Drowned in a tub?" he asked derisively. "You're bullshitting me."

"That's what the cops say. He died in his dead grandma's house in Belvington Heights late Thursday night. They say he was high on booze and downers and passed out in the tub.

But I think something else went down." I took a sip of coffee and glanced at him seductively over the rim of my cup.

He leaned back in the chair surveying me slowly, a smile playing on the edge of his lips. "So you think I killed this one, too?"

"I didn't say that."

"How well did you know him, this dead son of your ex-husband?"

"Not well," I said. If you didn't count the couple of times I'd seen Gerard as a kid, that few minutes I'd had with him on Emma's porch was about it.

"If you knew him at all, you'd know he was the kind of slimy little son of a bitch who deserved to drown himself in somebody's tub."

I'd said similar words to his mama, of all people, not four days ago myself, but the sneer on Basil's face as he said those words sent a chill through me.

"Don't you have any respect for anything, even the dead?" I asked, sounding more sanctimonious than I meant to.

"Not the dead that deserve to die."

"Who deserves to die that young?"

"Some of those who do."

"You don't mean that." I didn't mention Bettina, but I knew by the pain in his eyes and the way they shifted away from mine that he knew who I was referring to. But I also felt reassured. Would he show such feeling so easily for a "dead" sister who was still alive?

"Let's not speak of death," he said with an exaggerated poetic flair.

"Death has been what I've been dealing with for the last week. There's nothing else I want to talk about. What did you mean when you said that mess about Carlotta?" I added. "The stuff about her fucking people, anything in britches, like an alley cat?"

"Just what it sounds like," he said. He took a sip of coffee. "She, Carlotta, had been fucking Gerard for the past year. Terrence knew it. Gerard knew he knew it. Carlotta knew he knew it. And now you know it," he finished the revelation with an amused grin.

I stared at him, in disbelief. "Gerard was twenty years old. Carlotta is a grown woman," I said. "The same age as me when Jamal was born. Why would a grown woman like that be messing around with a twenty-year-old kid?"

"She's twenty-two, Tamara. The same age as you when we first met—" He paused for effect and then continued. "Two years, maybe even less, older than him. Since when is a twenty-two-year-old woman a grown woman to a twenty-year-old man? When I was twenty, I had women twice, three times my age . . . well, maybe ten years," he added with a sheepish grin.

"But Gerard?" I asked again. He shrugged as if saying it was beyond his understanding too.

"Maybe she saw something you don't," he

said, explaining. "You know what they used to say in the Seventies, 'Different strokes for different folks.' And maybe he was putting down some strokes she didn't know could be swam."

"I don't know," I said, still not convinced. But then again, I thought to myself, it could explain the violent argument I'd heard that day on the porch between Emma and Gerard. For all I knew, the last words that had been spoken between them had been about him seeing and sleeping with somebody she didn't want him to see. No names had been called, but what if it was Carlotta? "How do *you* know about it?" I asked Basil.

"Everybody knew it. Gerard had a big mouth. He made that fool of an ex-husband of yours a laughingstock in every circle he ran in. Everybody was laughing at him. From the waiters who pour his Scotch in that shitty club off Bradford where he hangs, to that weird little secretary who answers his phone. Him spending money on that little tramp like she was the Princess of Wales. Her fucking his son behind his back in his own mama's house every time she could get her hands on him. It's funny as hell if you think about it!" He gave a malicious guffaw of contempt.

"Did DeWayne know?" I asked, listening closely to everything he said, adding things to the list I had in my mind.

"Who would tell him? When you get something like that on a man like DeWayne, you keep it to yourself, savor it, laugh about it behind his back. It was a standing joke. Nobody cares about him enough to tell him shit."

"And Terrence knew?"

"Word was that somebody was paying him *not* to tell DeWayne. Before he died, Terrence was throwing money around like he'd won the lottery. He was getting the money from somebody. Gerard was doing some light coke deals with some high school kids, so he had money. But it could have been Carlotta, too. She milked that fool DeWayne Curtis like a cow. A cash cow."

I got up to pour some more coffee in our cups, and then sat back down across from him, my knee gently brushing his under the table; he pressed his firmly against mine.

"Basil, why are you telling me all this?" *What is in this for you?*

"What is it with you, woman? Has no one ever told you not to look a gift horse in the mouth? You don't take gifts offered? Or keep promises made?" he added. "You know what I want to tell you: come back with me now to my place."

I studied his face carefully: the amused smile, the dark eyes that could glow with either desire or deception—*bedroom eyes* my grandma used to call them—the wide, soft lips so sensually turned. Could this face that I found so bewitching be that of a killer?

I paused for a moment, considering it for the briefest second, and then remembered it was Sunday afternoon; Basil was not the kind of man you invite to Sunday dinner.

"Not today," I said.

"When?" he asked. He shifted slightly in his seat, and I noticed the bulge of a .38 concealed unsuccessfully in the folds of his expensive leather jacket. His eyes widened slightly, telling me he knew that I'd noticed it.

"I'm not sure if I want to go anywhere with a man who carries a gun."

"You were a cop; you have one."

"I hate guns," I said, and I meant it.

"Mine is licensed," he added. "I need it for protection."

"Protection? From who?"

"Women like you, who can see through lies. So I am seduced and abandoned," he added with a self-mocking grin. "You've got what you want from me and now you leave me to pine away in despair and rejection."

"Basil, you and I both know that you never have and never will pine away in despair and rejection—for me or any woman."

"You know me less well than you think, Tamara Hayle," he said. He drank the last of his coffee and stood up, straightening his jacket to conceal the gun more successfully. Then he stopped, placed a soft, playful kiss on my lips and turned to leave.

But that kiss, lingering on the soft inner

edges of my mouth, made my body remember the first time his lips had touched mine, and last Friday, and then all the times I'd wanted to run the tip of my tongue over the full, curving lines that formed his mouth.

Desire happens with no warning or reflective moment, no time to run into the bathroom and brush your teeth or spray FDS where you think it will matter. When I thought about it later, I realized that Basil was as unprepared as I was for what happened next, for this "act of nature" that swept us like a violent downpour, the kind that leaves you clutching your clothes and running for cover. But we didn't run.

The sexual fever between us this time was not the leisurely seduction of Friday night, the lingering of lips on face and throats and breasts. It was a flash fire that struck us as hot and quick as anything I've ever known. Yet there was a tenderness mingled with the heat of his lips as they swept me into a frenzy of desire for him.

He took off his jacket first, placing it on the table away from us. I remembered the gun, stopped short, but then his kisses came so quickly and with such fervor that in a moment all thoughts of it were gone. We were undressed before I knew it, tossing our clothes in a heap on the floor around us. His body was strong and hard as ebony. I ran my fingers and lips down the curve of his back and across his chest for the pure delight of touching him, feeling his skin against the tips of my fingers and tasting his warm salty body with my tongue. He kissed my breasts, my arms, my neck, the inside of my thighs, on and within everywhere I imagined they could go.

But the doubt lingered. *Could Basil be the killer?* That thought and the sudden hardness of the kitchen floor snapped me back to reality. Basil sensed my coolness and pulled away.

"What's wrong?"

"Nothing," I murmured, catching my breath and pulling down my sweatshirt.

"Do you want to go upstairs?"

I thought for a moment. Would making love to Basil in my bedroom really ease my mind? Granted, it would certainly make it more acceptable. There was, after all, the very real possibility that my teen-age son would pop in here, where he routinely gobbled down peanut butter sandwiches as he watched *The Simpsons*, and find his mother rolling around on the kitchen floor with the man who had cursed his father out at his dead brother's funeral. I cringed at the thought.

"Was it that bad?" Basil asked with an amused grin as he watched me, reading my discomfort but not my thoughts.

"No. It's not that," I said quickly. He kissed me again on the throat, right above my collarbone, one of those "love spots" that always get me going, and a thrill went through me as my body drifted back into his. But I pulled back as his lips touched mine and his hand gently stroked my breasts.

Was my hesitancy some instinct about danger that I was following?

"I'm really not a tease," I said after a minute. "I guess you think that I am, after this, after last Friday. But I'm not."

"Did I say that?" he asked as he drew back slightly and surveyed me with an amused glint in his eye. "Maybe you're just a woman who doesn't let herself get caught up in the moment."

"The truth is that I'm not any more sure about what is between us than I was on Friday," I said, deciding that I owed him the truth. "Maybe less sure."

"I'm risking as much as you are." He stood up and gave me his hand. I pulled myself up to face him, less gracefully than I wished. "Women never understand that about men. The risk cuts both ways, not just one. I am as much in your power as you are in mine."

We sat back down at the table, facing each other. Back to square one.

"Is it something to do with DeWayne?" he asked after a minute. "You think I have something to do with those boys dying?"

"I didn't say that."

"You don't have to."

"Basil . . ."

"Make up your mind, my love," he said, after a minute. "And a piece of advice for you: Don't let killers into your home." He said it with a bitter turn in his voice that made me cringe. "I'm a poor loser."

"Basil, it's not about losing or winning. Will we see each other again?" I asked, as he pulled on his jacket, the notion of the gun catching my attention for a fraction of a moment. The moment I said it I hated the way it sounded, and if I could have pulled the words back I would have.

He paused. "That's up to you," he said. "When you've decided who I am. Good-bye, Tamara," he said softly and kissed me again on *that* spot on my neck. I couldn't trust my voice to come out normal so I didn't say anything.

After he'd gone, I sat looking at my cup half-filled with coffee. Then I picked it up and absentmindedly took a sip. It was cold now, and bitter. I spit it back into the cup. *Should we have gone upstairs? What harm would it have done? I was a grown woman with the right to do with my life and libido what I wanted to.*

I was suddenly swept with a sense of regret so strong that I nearly called out his name. *Would it be right next time?* Why at this point in my life did I always have to be so damn cautious, so careful with my loving? I'd never been one of those women to simply cast my fate to the wind and just let life happen to me. I cursed myself for my caution.

I felt like a cigarette. Something to get rid of the tension, to help me clear my mind.

But as it ended up, I didn't have time to think too hard about missing a cigarette or even a roll on the kitchen floor with Basil. Jamal and Hakim came bounding into the house, all laughter and thumping basketballs.

"Did the guy who tried to beat Daddy up at the funeral just leave here?" Jamal demanded to know as he dribbled into the kitchen. "We saw him leaving when we were coming out of Warren's. What was he doing here?"

I immediately knew I'd made the right decision. "Put the ball away. No," I lied. "That wasn't the same guy. He's a friend of mine, if it's any of your business."

I turned away, my eyes frantically searching the kitchen for any sign of our near lovemaking. I wondered if any trace was left on my face. Jamal studied me closely.

"How good a friend?" he asked protectively.

"Listen, son," I said, emphasizing the word "son," and putting every stern stroke of authority that I could into my voice. "I don't need a fourteen-year-old overdosing on his own testosterone watching my back. Thanks but no thanks for your concern about my social life. You have friends that I don't know. I have friends that you don't know. Let's leave it at that. Mind your business, honey. Don't you all have something to do?" I asked, turning to confront him and Hakim with an arched eyebrow of dismissal.

Jamal gave me a smile. "OK, Mom. But when I have some phat girlie leaving the house when you're not home, don't be saying nothing." Hakim chuckled and slapped him five.

"Leave it alone, fellas," I said in a voice that let them know I meant business. Jamal shrugged a suit-yourself shrug, popped a bag of Orville Redenbacher popcorn in the microwave, and he and Hakim headed into the living room to watch some videos. I sat down and made myself a cup of peppermint tea, still savoring the taste of Basil on my lips as I drank it.

"Can I stay here tonight, Aunt Tam?" Hakim asked a couple of hours later when I called Jamal to set the table for dinner. Hakim was the only person besides Jake I let call me "Tam." He'd added the "Aunt" a year ago, deciding, he said, that it was time to show me some respect. "Will you cook something in the wok?" He was also the only kid I knew who actually liked the stuff I stir-fry in my ancient, mostly unused wok.

"Naw, man," Jamal said to him with disgust. "Don't nobody feel like eating nothing out of that wok."

"Shut up, Jamal. Yeah, Hakim, you can stay," I said. "Call your grandma, and we'll do the wok, but you've got to chop. I hate to chop."

He called his grandmother and then joined me in the kitchen about twenty minutes later. As he chopped celery, onions and a couple of mushrooms that had sat unused in the fridge for about a week, he ran his mouth about basketball, how he liked chemistry but didn't want to tell anybody, and how he was trying to play the trumpet like Wynton Marsalis—the kinds of things he never told Jamal because Jamal was too young, nor his grandma because she was too old.

But I only half listened, my mind was on Basil and what had nearly happened between us and what he had told me, and it stayed there while I stir-fried the chicken, fixed some rice, watched *Roc* and *The Sunday Night Movie* and finally curled up under my down comforter ready to go to sleep. When the phone rang, I didn't answer until the fourth ring, right before the machine comes on. I half hoped it was Basil. But it was Jake.

"You sleep?"

"No, not really."

"Did Jamal tell you I called?"

"That jive little Negro never tells me squat. But I was going to call you tomorrow. Did you hear about Gerard?" I sat up, almost awake now.

"Yeah, I heard over at the station. What the hell is going on, Tam?"

"I don't know. I found out something today though that may be part of the puzzle." I told him all the things Basil had told me earlier and the official word on how Terrence had died. I didn't mention my adventure on the kitchen floor.

"So you think someone could do that—see to it that Terrence would have a severe-turned-fatal allergy attack?" Jake asked.

"Yeah. It seems farfetched that somebody would go that far, think up a scheme so complicated, but, yeah, I think it could have gone down that way."

"Why not just shoot him?"

"They wanted it to seem like an accident so the cops wouldn't get into it. They knew he was a junkie, and that no one really gives a shit about junkies."

"So you agree with DeWayne?" Jake asked.

"I don't know," I said. "I don't think it's what DeWayne is saying, like a conspiracy or anything, but I think it was indirectly related to him."

"But why?"

"That depends on who."

"So how did they get in?"

"They could have told Miss Lee to let them in, saying they knew him. They could have been dressed as a delivery person. Hell, it could be somebody who knew him, and they just picked up the pills and gave them to him as a favor. It's not that hard to get into somebody's place, if you want to do it."

I paused. "I don't think he bought those flowers himself; I've been meaning to check to see if they were delivered, but it probably would be a waste of time. Anybody could have picked them up in any supermarket—the A&P, Pathmark, anywhere, they have all the flowers you can buy. They might have been a gift from somebody, something that he accepted out of courtesy and then threw away, and that could mean he knew the person and didn't want to hurt his or her feelings. Terrence was a pretty decent kid in a lot of ways, and they knew that about him too. Whoever it was knew him well enough to know he probably had allergies, or they knew DeWayne that well, and knew it ran in his family."

"How much cocaine would it have taken to kill him?"

"A teaspoon. But maybe it wasn't cocaine alone. Maybe something was mixed with it to make it fatal," I said.

"There could be something in that, Tam," he said, sounding as if he were turning something over in his mind. "We had a case a couple of years back where somebody ground up some hemlock stems."

"Hemlock?"

"You can find it around—it's native to Eurasia and Africa, but if you know where to look, you can find it. Anyway, the perp put it in some brownies with acid—LSD. Brother thought he was tripping and tripped himself right into the cemetery. It's like curare, paralyzes your muscles. There's a lot of pain, but if you're tripping you don't feel it. Respiratory paralysis is the cause of death. Acid does strange things to people. That's what the coroner said. But the vic's mama swore he was poisoned, and when we tested him for it later, that's what we found: hemlock. So poison mixed with something else might be a possibility."

I was fully awake now. I could hear Jamal and Hakim still listening to MTV down in the living room. I got up and closed my door and climbed back into the bed.

"Terrence was throwing money around before he died," I said.

"What if he was blackmailing Gerard and Carlotta? If the money came from one of them," Jake said, staying with the conversation. I lay in my bed, listening. "That would explain the money you found in his refrigerator. It also explains why Gerard and Carlotta weren't exactly grieving at Terrence's wake. Did they both have opportunity? They had motives, particularly Carlotta. Tell me what you know about her."

"Twenty-two. Pretty. Hell, you've seen her, gorgeous in a tacky kind of way," I added. "Carlotta Lee is her maiden name. Her aunt was Terrence's landlady."

"So it would be simple for her to have access. What's her aunt's name?"

"Miss Lee is all I know."

"Cleotha Lee?" Jake asked.

"Cleotha? I don't know. God, who would name a child Cleotha?"

"It's one of those good old Southern names they used to hang on helpless kids back in the day. Don't knock it. I got a sweet old cousin on my daddy's side named Cleotha."

"Who is Cleotha Lee?" I asked.

"About twenty or so years ago, Cleotha Lee used to launder money for the mob. Bought up property after the riots, bought it cheap, sold it cheap. Gave seed money to small-time baby hoodlums like your ex. Dealt a little coke and weed when coke was 'recreational' and everybody was getting high. Nothing big-time, penny-ante stuff, but it kept her in furs and wigs."

"Do you think she knew DeWayne back then? I know he came north, to Newark, in the early Seventies, right after the riots."

"He may have. There's a lot about that brother you don't know, Tam. Do you think he knew about Carlotta and Gerard?"

"I think he might have suspected something," I said, remembering the strange look in DeWayne's eyes when DeLorca asked him if he knew how Gerard had gotten into his mother's locked house.

158

"Do you think DeWayne could have killed Terrence?" Jake asked bluntly.

"No, Jake! DeWayne is many things but he's not a killer!" I said, surprising myself at my defense of DeWayne.

"Jealousy, a brother's passion for his pretty young wife, will make him do many things, Tamara. Maybe Carlotta killed Terrence. Then DeWayne killed Gerard."

"DeWayne wouldn't kill his own son, Jake. He'd throw Carlotta out in the street before he'd do that."

"Maybe Miss Lee had something on him that would make that impossible. I don't know. Maybe he didn't go over there meaning to kill Gerard, maybe things just got out of hand," Jake added persistently.

"Then why would he keep paying me to find a killer?"

"He asked you to do it before Gerard was dead."

"Then why hasn't he called me off?"

"Maybe he will."

"DeWayne didn't do anything to Gerard, Jake. That killing wasn't the kind you do from passion. Somebody drowned him in the tub, a sneaky, premeditated kind of murder. And that's another thing, how do you drown a grown man in a tub?"

"It was one of those old-fashioned, claw-footed jobs with the sloping back, right?"

"How did you know?"

"Ever bathe in one of those things, Tam? We used to have one in my mother's place. Somebody's relaxing in one of those tubs, back up against the slope, eyes closed, coolin' out, high on weed or wine and, wham, it's easy. You grab their ankles and give them a yank. Head goes under the water. Sides are too slippery to grab them and pull yourself back up. There's nothing you can do but drown, long as they hold you down. Nothing. Whoosh! You're dead meat."

I thought about it for a moment. "It's not a man's way to kill."

"Getting sexist, are we?" Jake asked with a chuckle. "Anybody who will kill somebody will kill them any way they can. Maybe if Carlotta killed Terrence to stop some blackmailing, maybe she killed Gerard too."

I thought about that. Carlotta seemed pretty cold, but would she kill her lover? "Why would she kill Gerard?"

"Maybe she was tired of him. Maybe she had to prove something to DeWayne. Maybe DeWayne threatened to do something to her or told her she was in danger some way."

"Why would that be so important to her?"

"Your guess is as good as mine. And I'll tell you something else, don't rule out your boy Basil in all of this."

My heart stopped. "What do you mean, *my* boy Basil?" I asked, all of my feelings—the

160

passion, the contradiction, the doubts—coming out in my voice.

He didn't quite answer my question. "Be careful, that's all I'm saying." He said it in a big-brother tone I hadn't heard from him in years, but there was another edge to it. Was it jealousy? I wondered.

"He's not *my* boy, Jake. What do you know about him?"

"Nothing. But word is he can't go home because he killed somebody in the Islands. There's a guy in my office whose brother grew up in the same place outside Kingston. Says Basil killed the guy who killed his father. Vendetta. Like the Italians in their little towns in Sicily. Revenge. It's big with guys like Basil, honor and all that shit."

Revenge. My stomach sank. Bettina.

"I guess you could say he had a grudge against DeWayne," I said slowly. But Jake hardly heard me. He was on a roll.

"Word has it that he has some light interest in the coke scene. Gerard was a light dealer too."

"Have you ever heard that Basil had a sister, Bettina?" I asked cautiously.

"No, what about her?"

"I heard that DeWayne was responsible for her becoming a hooker, for her death." *"I heard . . ." I was protecting him.*

"Turning out whores isn't DeWayne's style," Jake said.

VALERIE WILSON WESLEY

"Do you think Basil could have something to do with Gerard or Terrence?" I asked. My heart had started to beat fast, and I hoped that Jake couldn't hear the fear in my voice.

He paused a few moments before he answered, as if he was thinking about something. "If he does, it's more than you can handle, Tam, stay out of it. Gerard and Terrence were both first-class losers. I don't mean to be talking ill of the dead, but neither of them young brothers was headed toward nothing but trouble."

"I know. But I'm still afraid, Jake. What if we're wrong about this having to do with Carlotta or Basil. What if it's going to touch Jamal more than it has." I whispered like a kid might, as if saying it aloud would make it happen. "It just scares the shit out of me."

"Tamara, you know I'm here for you, anytime day or night you need me," Jake said to me in that strong, assured voice that makes me feel like a little girl curling up to her tough, warm daddy.

"I'm scared to death, Jake."

"Whatever went down, it has everything to do with Terrence and Gerard, nothing to do with you and Jamal," Jake said firmly, using the big-brother voice I heard him use with Jamal when he needed comforting, trying to be assuring.

"Possibly Carlotta, Miss Lee, DeWayne, Basil—they're all tied up in it somehow. Tam,

162

you're not listening to me," Jake said firmly. "This is DeWayne's mess, whatever it is. Something to do with his pretty young wife and her crooked old aunt, and his thug of an ex-partner." I cringed when he said that. *Thug of an ex-partner that I'd almost made love to on my kitchen floor. Or was it fucked?*

"—nothing to do with you," Jake continued. "Nothing to do with Jamal. Why don't you call DeWayne tomorrow and tell him you're out of it?"

I stopped short. That had never occurred to me until he said it. When I get involved with something, I don't like to let it go.

"What do you mean, tell him I'm out of it?"

"Just what I said."

"I don't want to give up that easily."

"Take what you've come up with, everything that you think went down and talk it over with DeLorca. I'll run it by some guys in the Department that I know and see if you can get some official weight behind it to really look into things.

"Tam, I don't like the way you're sounding. I can't remember the last time I heard you scared, and I don't like it. Make me a promise. Promise me you'll give it one more day. Until tomorrow. One more day and then you'll send DeWayne a bill and let it go. OK?"

"I don't know."

"Stay out of it, Tam. You probably shouldn't have gotten involved with this mess in the first place. The death of DeWayne's first son was a coincidence. His guilt is sending him through changes. Gerard and Terrence were involved in something—Gerard making it with his daddy's old lady and not having the good sense to keep quiet about it. Terrence knowing his brother couldn't keep his drawers on and not having the good sense to keep quiet about it. Big mouths, raging hormones and shameless greed has done in many a good man, and those two guys weren't good.

"That's the end of it, Tam. Let it go. You're starting to get involved with DeWayne again. You're getting drawn back into his life, that dude is like quicksand, like fucking quicksand. You've actually begun to feel sorry for his sorry ass again, and that worries me. Let DeWayne and his fucked-up problems go their own way. Don't get trapped by him again, do you hear me?"

"Jake, I'm not a fool. You know I'm not about to get involved with DeWayne again. How could you say something like that?"

"I know you, Tam. If there's some loser with an interesting, dangerous edge to him you're probably going to fall in love with him before the month is out."

"Jake. I resent that. How could you say something like that to me?" I was angry because I knew he was right. Angry at him because it probably should have been him instead of Basil, and if it had been, everything

164

would be all right. But it wasn't, and it probably never would be. "Jake, just leave me the fuck alone!" I said like an angry kid. I felt tears coming to my eyes, for everything that was out of control in my life.

"Tam, you're tired, let it go," Jake said gently. "Promise me this: One more day and then you write up your suspicions about how Terrence died, and my theory about the claw-foot tub and the whole mess we've been talking about tonight, and you take it to DeLorca. Tell him you don't know who did it, or *if* anyone did, but you suspect—bam, bam, bam, finish, out of here."

"He won't care," I said, but my thoughts were on Basil and what had almost happened and the fact that despite it all, the doubts were rising again.

"Listen. Despite your feelings about cops, and I'm not saying it's not justified, some of them actually do care about catching the bad guys—or girls as the case may be. And one of the cops who care is DeLorca, you know that as well as me."

Jake was right about DeLorca, and he was right about my being tired, too. Gerard's death coming so soon after Terrence's had unnerved me. Who did I think I was, trying to catch a murderer—if there even had been a murder? Maybe Jake was right. Take my thoughts to DeLorca and talk them over with him. Jake had hit on one indisputable truth: DeWayne was in my life more than I needed him to be. And now there was Basil. I was tired, and sick of the whole mess.

"OK," I agreed after about a minute and a half of running it around in my mind. "I'll call DeLorca."

"And DeWayne?"

"I'll tell him what's up tomorrow when I go to work."

"Go to sleep, Tam."

"OK, Jake," I sighed. "One more day, I promise," I added more to myself than to him, and when I hung up I meant it.

I never knew exactly what Wyvetta Green would look like from day to day. The constants were she was tall and thin, with skin as smooth as molasses and an easy smile. But she was the only sister I knew who changed hairdos like most folks change clothes. When I walked into Jan's Beauty Biscuit late the next morning, her hair was piled high on her head à la Marge Simpson, and she'd dyed the ends a strange color of brown gone burnt orange. Some days she could carry off these 'dos like nobody's business, but on others even her boyfriend, loud-mouthed Earl Elam, would do a double take. This was one of those days.

"Like it?" Wyvetta asked as I stepped into the Biscuit.

"Well, Wyvetta, to tell the truth..."

"Ain't nobody asked you to tell the truth, go on and lie like everybody else!" she said with a twinkle in her eye as she carefully combed a white foaming substance through a dubious customer's hair. "What you doing coming in here so late? You're lucky you don't have to work like everybody else. Some heifers have all the luck! This lady is a detective. A bona-fide private eye," she added, waving her comb in my direction to her customer held captive. "If somebody owes you money or hats with your last half-dollar, this here's the sister to track them down."

I acknowledged her compliment with a nod, and the customer looked me over with renewed respect.

Wyvetta turned back to her task, shifting away from the fumes of the chemicals she was applying. "So what you doing stepping in here at noon?"

"Overslept."

"Overslept?" she asked, the question dripping with innuendo. "Most folks do their 'oversleeping' on Friday and Saturday nights!"

"Get your mind out the gutter, Wyvetta. I was working yesterday when you were still cuddling up to Earl. I'm making up for those lost Z's."

"When?" Wyvetta asked, as she wiped, with a motherly flourish, spots of foam from her customer's cheek. "I came in at two to catch up on my books." She looked up at me and threw me a grin. "I've been coming in here every Sunday, *every* Sunday, to keep my records straight so I won't have to be paying no fool to do my taxes in April. What time were you here?"

"About six or seven in the morning," I answered, sorting through the letters and assorted flyers from our shared mailbox.

"Six or seven! Well, forget you, and you can just put them bills right back where you found them. I don't feel like no bad luck today." Wyvetta pouted as I handed her several letters. "Like old Eviliene in *The Wiz* says: Don't be bringing me no bad luck. Like my grandma used to say, If I didn't have bad news, I'd have no news at all." Wyvetta loved to quote folks one on top of the other, even though she almost always got the quotes wrong.

"Wyvetta, it's if I didn't have bad *luck*, I'd have no luck at all."

"Speaking of bad news, girl," she said, ignoring my correction. "You got some visitors this morning. Guess who walked in here this morning when I opened the door? Your ex. And guess who came strolling in ten minutes after he left? Mrs. Carlotta Lee Curtis!"

"DeWayne and Carlotta? *Both* looking for me?"

"Yeah. I'm always glad to see Carlotta. She's definitely my girl with her five-hundred-dollar weave! But girlfriend was looking bad this morning, like something evil was gnawing at her."

I was right. Wyvetta did do Carlotta's

weave. I'd get the dirt on the girl later on, after she'd closed shop.

"Your ex? I don't know what he wanted," Wyvetta continued. "That's one good-looking man, though. He can ride me in that pretty silver Lexus anytime he feels like it!"

"Um-hum!" grunted the captive customer in agreement.

"Wyvetta, don't wish too hard for something like that, you just might get it," I said sourly. "What did they say before they left?"

"Well, Mr. Fine-ass, Lexus-driving De-Wayne said to ask you to call him at home soon as you can. *She* said she'd call you later on today."

"Thanks, Wyvetta, I'll check you later on," I said as I dropped Wyvetta's mail on a nearby counter and headed up the stairs fast.

Both? I could understand DeWayne, but both of them? The phone rang before I could take off my coat.

"Where the fuck have you been?" DeWayne asked impatiently.

I froze. In the space of five seconds, he'd managed to erase any bit of good will I'd developed for him during our talk late Friday night when he'd come over to be with Jamal after they found Gerard's body.

"Who the fuck do you think you're talking to?" I snapped back with as much venom as I could spew without upsetting my stomach. "Have you lost your mind talking to me like that? I'm not your damn wife anymore."

"Jesus. I'm sorry, Tammy. I didn't mean it to come out sounding like that. You know I don't talk to you like that. You know I *never* talked to you like that, except maybe once or twice. This shit has been coming down on me so fast and hard, I can't even think straight anymore. I can't even talk decently to a decent woman."

"And don't call me Tammy," I added, still mad.

"I'm sorry, Tamara. Can we talk for a minute? Emma doesn't want to have a funeral for Gerard. She's going to cremate him," he said, not waiting for me to answer him. "He was her son more than mine anyway. That's how I feel about it. I'm too tired to fight her. She's going to have a memorial, just for a few people, she says. I'm going to bring Jamal with me, if that's OK with you."

"Fine, just let him know."

"I threw that little slut I was married to out my house this morning," he added as if it were an afterthought, something he'd just remembered.

He found out about her and Gerard, I thought to myself. "Why?" I feigned innocence. "Last Friday, you said—"

"I know what I said. But it's over now. Is there any way I can see you so we can talk in person? Maybe for a drink somewhere? Maybe dinner later on?"

"Before we go any further with this, there's something I have to talk to you about," I said. "I've been doing some thinking about everything that's been happening. I don't think I'm the person to look into this whole thing, I—"

"What do you mean?"

"There are things going on between you and your wife that I really would rather not get involved with. Between you, Carlotta, her aunt, Basil—"

"What does that old bitch have to do with anything, and Basil, that filthy son of a bitch, don't even say his name to me, Tamara. I don't owe him shit!"

"What about Bettina?"

Pause. "What about her?"

"I want out," I said finally. "I don't want to be involved anymore on any level. Today is my last day. Tomorrow morning I'm sending you my bill. I'd appreciate it if—"

"Are you telling me you are giving up? Are you saying you're not going to help me? You want more money? Is that what this is about?" he asked sharply.

"I want my peace of mind back," I said, my voice rising now. "Money can't buy that, DeWayne. This isn't feeling right to me, not like the kind of thing I want to do. This whole mess has gotten bad for my nerves."

"Bad for your nerves? Bad for *your* goddamned nerves? What about my nerves,

Tamara? What about me? Damn, you bitches, it's always about you, isn't it?''

"Fuck you, DeWayne," I said, my blood pressure over the top, pissed that he'd managed to push my button again. "Just send me my damn—"

"Wait, please, Tamara, please," he said, begging, something I rarely heard him do. "Jesus, I'm sorry, Tamara. On my mother's grave, I'm sorry! Just listen to me for another minute."

"What?"

"My boys, Tamara, all my boys."

"Sons you never really thought about till they started dying."

"OK," he said. "Maybe that's part of it. Maybe it's because I feel like shit about this. Maybe it's because I *am* shit because of it, because I haven't been there for them like I should have. But that means I owe them, Tamara. I owe them to find out who is doing this. Please, please help me."

"Get somebody else."

"I can't. You know the kind of shit I've been involved in all my life. The number of people I can trust number about four, and one of them, my mama, is dead. The second one, you, well, you know where things stand between us now. And that cunt I was married to, I just threw out. For all I know *she* could have killed Terrence. She had a good enough reason to do it, that's for goddamn sure."

He definitely knew about Carlotta and Gerard,

173

and about Terrence, too. My call-waiting line clicked.

"I've got to take this call," I said. "I'll get right back to you." I clicked over, eager to get away. A whispery, sad little voice floated over the other end. *Carlotta*.

"Miss Hayle," she said, "I wanted to know if I could make an appointment to talk to you later on today?" *Miss Hayle?* What was that mess? But Wyvetta was right. She sounded bad.

"Carlotta, can you tell me what this is about?" I asked.

"I can't talk about it now, on the phone. I'm staying with my aunt over on Avon. Could you come over here? Could we talk over here?" She sounded like a kid, and I was having a hard time fitting what I knew about her with the helpless, little-girl voice I heard. I'd told DeWayne I was sick of this case—of him, his problems—and I was. I wanted things to go back to the way they were—him calling me once every couple of months to hook up with Jamal and staying out of my life. But as it always did, my curiosity was getting the better of me. It was always my downfall. I decided I owed Terrence today. *One more day*.

"About an hour?" I asked Carlotta.

"Yeah. If you talk to my husband, don't tell him I called you," she added quickly, and hung up.

I clicked back over to DeWayne.

"Can you give me another week?" De-Wayne asked.

"I've made up my mind."

"Have it your own goddamn way," he said and hung up.

13

I had come full circle. I was back where I started, standing on the front porch of Miss Lee's house, and it seemed as fitting a place as any to end things. I thought about Terrence and his small bare room at the top of the stairs; guilt swept me. "Let it go," I said to myself. "Just let it go." *Had I done right by him?* I'd done what I could. This was DeWayne's debt to pay, not mine.

I wondered whether I should tell Carlotta about leaving the case, then decided I wouldn't bother. She'd find out soon enough. Curiosity had brought me here, and curiosity had to be satisfied. I rang the doorbell once and then again for good measure. Carlotta came before the bell stopped chiming.

She was wearing black leggings that made her legs look thinner than they had in heels, and a grungy black sweatshirt with a picture of Mike Tyson and the words "Free Him" stamped across the front. Her hair was bunched into a thick ponytail that hung limply down her back, and from the looks of it Wyvetta would be counting my girl's money sooner rather than later. The dime-sized diamond earrings she'd worn to Terrence's wake had been replaced by small gold "door knocker" hoops. Gone too were the eye shadow, blusher and glossy red lipstick of last Tuesday night. Her face looked colorless and pinched; her eyes were red. All in all, she looked like a heartbroken sixteen-year-old.

"Thank you for coming," she said in a small polite voice.

"I'm just glad to be of help," I answered in the subdued, phony professional tone I use on occasions like this. The foyer didn't look much better than it had during last week's rain. The sun broke through the dusty blinds in several places, but the hall still looked like it needed a good paint job, and the same dilapidated umbrellas stood abandoned in the stand. We walked in silence down the dim, slightly dank foyer toward her aunt's apartment. She jingled a ring with about twelve keys on it, and then picked out two of them and quickly opened two deadbolt locks.

We stepped into a light-colored living room in which sunlight bounced off the walls and sparkled through immaculately clean windows—a stunning contrast to the dimness of the foyer—and in which the vague scent of lilac lingered in the air. Boston ferns hung from two windows, track lighting ran across the ceiling, and a couch, a long narrow number upholstered in beige velvet, snaked its way along the wall. Miss Lee hadn't seemed like the doily and African violet type, but I hadn't expected this decor either.

I'd always figured Carlotta was DeWayne's type of woman—a tough little bitch-on-wheels despite her age (though DeWayne's type of woman had never been what you'd expect—I could vouch for that). But today she seemed sadder and more vulnerable than I had ever seen her.

"Please sit down," she said with a nod toward the couch, and I sank down into it. She settled into a straight-backed chair directly across from me and reached for a cigarette from a half-filled pack of Newports, my old brand. I watched the cigarette leave the pack and followed its quick trail to her lips—the old habits of a former fiend die hard. Noting my interest, she shoved the pack across the coffee table in my direction.

"Want one?"

"No, thanks," I said. "I quit."

She glanced at me doubtfully and then struck a match, inhaled deeply and shook the flame out with a twist of her slender wrist.

"I guess you wonder why I called," she said.

"It crossed my mind."

"I need some information." I noticed that her bottom lip quivered slightly as she spoke. "DeWayne told me Sunday before last that he'd hired you, and I wanted to know if you'd found anything about who could have killed Gerard." She took two quick drags from the cigarette, her left foot tapping out a soft rat-a-tat rhythm on the brown shag rug beneath our feet. "If you want me to pay you, I will. I have money . . . I can get money, and I need to find out. I have my reasons." She shifted her eyes down to the coffee table and inhaled again on the cigarette, blowing out smoke in a slow stream.

"Why?" I asked.

"Why what?"

"Why do you need to find out, and what are your reasons?"

"What do you mean, why? He was my husband's son, isn't that enough? I want to know who killed him."

"The cops say Gerard drowned accidentally in the tub."

"I don't think you believe that. I've told you I'll pay you for the information." She averted her eyes. "I told you, I have money to pay you, apart from what you're getting from De-Wayne, and I have my reasons, ones that are none of your damn business." She added the last part with a nasty twist that surprised me because there was no reason for it; she'd called me.

"You've got a lot of reasons you don't want to go into," I said.

"Let's cut the bullshit," she said, her eyes latching onto mine and narrowing as she spoke—little girl pretending to be tough.

"Yeah, let's cut the bullshit," I said, narrowing my eyes, raising my voice, meeting her attitude with mine. "I know you were fucking Gerard. I know Terrence knew it. I know DeWayne knows it now and just threw you out, probably because of it, but it may have been because you and Gerard killed his son. I know Terrence is dead. I know Gerard is dead. I know somebody killed them both. I *don't* know who yet, so why don't *you* just cut the bullshit and tell *me* what this is all about."

I wasn't expecting what happened next, although if I'd been watching that foot tapping its soft staccato on the rug I would have seen it coming. Suddenly her shoulders collapsed, her head dropped down on her chest and she began to cry.

It wasn't the neat, prissy kind of crying you do to make somebody feel sorry for you, but the kind that starts deep in your throat, travels down through your gut and leaves your whole body shaking like you're having a fit. It was a cry of despair and grief so powerfully felt it brought tears to my eyes.

The truth is I've never been able to watch somebody cry without joining in. It happens when I watch a good *Movie of the Week* and every time I catch *The Color Purple*. I cry at weddings where I don't know the bride, and funerals where I don't know the corpse. Tears are my weakness, an annoying reflex that in the kind of "tough guy" work I'm supposed to be doing are as embarrassing as hell. And Carlotta crying hard like she was doing grabbed me deep where I grieve for every loss I've ever had. I watched her for about three minutes, and then reached out to her, touching her shoulder gently, to comfort her.

"My life is over. I have nothing now. You don't know," she muttered, shaking her head in despair. "You just don't know."

"What don't I know?" I asked, suddenly Sister Confessor.

"You don't know."

"Talk to me, Carlotta. You'll feel better if you just let it out."

"You don't know ... Nobody knows how much I love him."

"DeWayne?" I asked.

She looked at me as if I'd just spit on the rug.

"No! Not him. Gerard. I loved Gerard!"

"Gerard?" I asked, not disguising my surprise. It had never crossed my mind that Carlotta could actually *love* Gerard. I'd assumed that their thing was just something to get DeWayne's goat. I'd figured that DeWayne had been sleeping around, and she'd slept with his son, popping him the lowest blow she could deliver. But to actually *love* the boy? His own *mama* had had a hard time doing that.

"I had no idea," I said, with complete honesty.

"We were alike. We were more alike than anyone I've ever known, and now that he's gone I don't have anybody," she said. She had stopped crying now, but her voice didn't have any life to it.

"When did it happen? You and DeWayne have only been married about a year."

She nervously tugged on her hair and finally switched her ponytail to the front, between Mike Tyson's eyes, stroking it as if it had a life of its own. "We knew each other in school, actually I knew Terrence; we were about the same age, I was in his grade, and he introduced me to Gerard. It was before I married DeWayne."

"You were sleeping with Gerard before you married DeWayne?"

"We weren't sleeping together," she said, suddenly demure. "But we were friends. Gerard really didn't have a lot of friends."

I left that one alone. "When did things change?"

"You know, I started my marriage wanting it to work," she said defensively. I shrugged indifferently to dispel any thought that I cared one way or the other. She studied my face for a moment and then continued. "DeWayne's older than me. He's so much *older* than me."

"But you knew that when you married him."

"I thought I loved him when I married him. He seemed to have it all together. Everybody knew him. I thought everybody respected him. He had money. He always drove nice cars. He always dressed good. He looked good, and the fact that he was older made him seem smart. It was like he took care of me. And Cle liked him, she'd known him since he was a kid. She and his cousin, Delroy, used to go together back home in Virginia where they're from; Delroy and her were going to get married, then she left and came up here to make some money. She told me it would be a good thing for me to do."

"Cle?"

"My Aunt Cleotha."

So Jake was right. She was Cleotha Lee, and things between her and DeWayne definitely went back. I'd thought she looked familiar when I'd seen her here last week, but I couldn't place her. We must have met in some casual encounter during my DeWayne days.

"They had kind of worked out things between them. But nothing turned out like it was supposed to. Now Gerard is dead, and I'm back right here with my aunt where I started," Carlotta continued petulantly. As I listened, I could hear the young twenty-two-year-old kid she really was. Funny, when I thought about it, I'd married DeWayne at about the same age for about the same reasons.

"Your aunt *told* you to marry DeWayne? What did she have riding on your staying with him? Did she owe him something? Did he owe her?" I asked, not disguising my curiosity.

"She didn't exactly tell me, but I just know she wanted me to be with him, and I pretty much did what she told me to do most of the time," she said, sensing my interest and backing away.

"And then we got married, and he brought the kid, Hakim, to live with us, and the kid hated me because I wasn't his mother, and I hated the kid because he got in the way, and Gerard was there, looking good and being nice, and he couldn't stand DeWayne and couldn't stand his mother, and my aunt was starting to get on my nerves the same way, and we just did it."

We both sat there for a minute, listening to the sound of a radio playing somewhere upstairs in another apartment—"Love Me in a Special Way," an old tune by DeBarge that had come out during my marriage; for a moment my feelings came back—the fears, even the love I'd felt once for DeWayne. Old songs will do that to you if you let them.

"And then other things happened," Carlotta said quietly.

"What other things?" I asked, my attention drawn back to her.

"A couple of months after we got married, he started acting like something was eating at him. He started drinking hard, doing light coke, like he was trying to kill something inside him. And then he couldn't do it anymore." She said it bluntly with no attempt to be tactful or put a kindly twist on it—in a matter-of-fact, young-sister-speak-the-truth kind of voice.

"You mean do *it*?" I asked. The corners of Carlotta's lips turned up into a smirk. "You mean DeWayne was impotent?"

"I guess that's what they call it," she said with a shrug. "Impotent. He just couldn't do it anymore. And Gerard could do it good." We both paused, letting that one sit a minute.

"Did you ever find out what was wrong with him? Besides not being able to . . . do it, I mean," I asked finally, breaking the silence.

"You know what, I didn't know, I didn't try to find out, and I really didn't give a fuck," Carlotta said with finality. She got up and left the room, tossing her ponytail back to where it belonged.

DeWayne, impotent. It was funny in a way. Mr. Macho. Big-time Baby Maker couldn't get it up now with his twenty-two-year-old wife. I wanted to feel some glimmer of satisfaction at DeWayne's bad luck, some measure of black-woman-done-wrong-gets-revenge, but I couldn't. There was nothing, not even sadness. I wondered if it could all be tied up together, the loss of that first son, DeWayne, Jr., and his sudden impotence—his confrontation with death and his own mortality. Or was his weary dick finally screaming "No more! no more!" when confronted with the reality of a young, horny wife?

The latch turned on the deadbolt locks on the front door, and Miss Lee, holding two Pathmark bags topped with groceries, swooped into the room in all her tiny glory. She didn't see me at first as she bopped her head to the rhythm of some unidentifiable tune that she hummed loudly. She was dressed in a tan trench that looked like it came from Carlotta's closet, and a long midnight black wig curled up page-boy-style at the ends—à la Marilyn Quayle. I recognized her cologne—a loud lilac mixture—as the origin of the scent in the room. When she spotted me, she scowled and shoved the groceries onto a nearby table.

"What you want?" she snapped in much the same way that she had last Tuesday. Before I could tell her, Carlotta came back holding a can of beer, which she carefully placed down on the table.

"I told her to come," she said, answering for me and glaring defiantly at her aunt. Miss Lee turned her attention to Carlotta.

"Why did you do something stupid like that?" The undisguised hostility in her voice caught me short.

Carlotta threw her a studied blank look. "I wanted to ask her what she knows about Gerard."

"Nothing," Miss Lee said angrily, tossing her coat and bag on the table with the groceries. "She don't know nothing because there is nothing to know."

"You don't know that, Cle," Carlotta said.

"I know more than you think," Miss Lee replied.

"I loved him, Cle, you didn't. I want some answers," Carlotta said, facing her aunt down with a conviction that told me they'd had this talk before. Cleotha Lee looked at me and then quickly back at her niece like a mother telling a kid to shut up until the company has gone.

"You can just cut this shit out now!" she ordered. "I'm tired of this mess."

"You can't kill my feelings," Carlotta said. "You can kill a lot of things, Cle, but you can't kill my feelings."

"You ain't Erica Kane or Victoria Lord, you ain't one of them other soap opera queens you're always watching, why don't you just can the drama and get some damn self-respect and common sense? You better off with that boy dead. Go on and live your life like your daddy meant you to. Go back to your husband where you belong."

"Just because you don't have a life, just because you've forgotten how it feels to really feel anything or care about anybody. Just because you left your life down home, don't mean you have to take mine away," Carlotta said, her voice shaking with anger.

"I didn't leave nothing down there besides torn drawers and hard times," Miss Lee said, glaring at Carlotta. Then she turned to me, looking me up and down. I expected a tongue-lashing too, but instead she turned and picked up the groceries and headed to the kitchen. "Do what you want to do, girl. I'm tired of fooling with you," she said over her shoulder to Carlotta as she left. Carlotta opened the beer and took a sip of the foam that ran over to the side, licking the side of the can with a short little lick, like a cat.

"You want something to drink?" she asked.

"Too early for me," I said.

She chuckled, her mouth relaxing into a wide grin, the tension that had been there with her aunt suddenly gone. "You sound like Gerard," she said girlishly. "He never used to drink before three. I drink any old time I feel like it, but not Gerard. Sometimes he used to smoke weed or sometimes do some blow, but he never would drink before three." She had a faraway look as she spoke about him, sharing her memories with me.

"He seemed like a very sweet guy," I said, lying through my teeth.

"Yeah. He was special to me. We did a lot of things together. He taught me a lot of stuff even though he was younger."

"Like what?"

"Well—" She paused for a moment, remembering. "You know stuff you see on TV, funny stuff, like Bart Simpson and Beavis and Butt-Head? He taught me how to draw them." She giggled at the memory. "And he taught me how to mix drinks. Fancy ones like tequila sunrises and Black Russians and brandy Alexanders." She took a sip of beer as if sipping one of the drinks she'd just mentioned.

"Did he teach you to do drugs?" I asked bluntly.

She looked up, startled by my question, and for a second I didn't think she was going to reply.

"Kind of," she finally said. She lit another cigarette, inhaled, and spoke through the smoke. "We used to smoke weed together. He taught me how to tell good herb and how to roll a joint. But weed's not drugs, you know. It's not like he taught me to do other stuff. I don't do coke."

"Did he do other stuff?"

She shrugged. "I guess."

"They said he had barbiturates in him when he died," I said.

"That's just cops making up shit," she said scornfully. "When I left, he was just smoking weed." She gasped, taking in a short little breath, and looked guilty, her eyes like a kid who's been caught writing on the living room wall with lipstick. She glanced up at me to see if I had heard it. I had. She stamped out her newly lit cigarette and shifted her eyes from mine to the glimmer of ash in the ashtray.

"So you were with Gerard in DeWayne's mama's house the night he died?" I asked before the glow left the ash.

She paused for a moment. "Yeah."

"And he was alive when you left?"

"Yeah."

"Who had the keys to the house, you or him?"

"I had them."

"Did you go there a lot?"

"That's where we met."

"Where did you get the keys?"

"When we first started . . . you know, being together. After that first time, I remembered DeWayne's mother's house was empty, and I went to his office and got the extra set. DeWayne doesn't keep anything at home. He doesn't trust anybody. I had two sets made, then I put them back."

"You made Gerard a set?"

"Yeah, he asked me to, so I did."

"So he used the place too, to meet other people?"

She looked surprised. "I guess so. I never asked him. It was none of my business."

"Was he expecting somebody that night?"

"He was going out to meet somebody. Why are you asking me all these questions?" she asked suddenly, knitting her eyebrows together anxiously. "I haven't done anything wrong. And anyway you're not a cop."

"I know," I said. "But it will help you feel better, Carlotta, if you talk about it." That was a damn lie, but it sounded good, and she took the bait. I paused for a moment before I continued, making my voice sound familiar, warm, instant intimacy. "What was he doing when you left?" I asked.

She sighed, giving in. "I told you, I left him sitting in the tub smoking a joint. We'd just gotten out of bed, messing around. He took a bath because the shower was broke. He said he had a meeting later on."

"And he didn't do any other drugs?"

She looked away, avoiding my eyes again. "He may have done something. Sometimes if he wanted to stay cool, he took things, if he was upset and he wanted to be cool, but I don't know what kind. Maybe he did, but I left him sitting in the tub smoking weed."

"What time was that?"

"Around eleven-thirty. I remember because DeWayne was coming home at midnight, and I wanted to be there before he got home."

"The cops say he died at eleven-fifty. Was anybody else in the house?"

"Nobody else had keys, except DeWayne."

"And Gerard was alive when you left him?"

She sucked on her cigarette, taking it in a short, fast toke like it was a joint. "You're making me feel like I killed him! I told you that already," she said, her voice rising.

"*Did* you kill him, Carlotta?"

"Damn you! Leave me alone! Why are you doing this to me? But I'll tell you something, I don't care anymore. If the cops know I was there and think I killed him, I don't care, because it's like I'm dead anyway." She didn't cry this time, but the pain was there, and I stopped for a minute, and then started again more gently.

"Maybe the cops are right, maybe he just drowned like they said."

She shrugged. "Maybe they are," she said quietly, changing her tune.

"I found three hundred bucks—in Terrence's refrigerator when I came here last week," I said, shifting topics. "Do you know how he could have gotten it?"

She looked surprised. "No," she answered, her voice empty.

"Do you think Gerard could have given it to him to keep him quiet about you two?"

"I gave Terrence the goddamn money, now leave my niece alone!" said Miss Lee as she stomped into the living room from the kitchen, catching both me and Carlotta by surprise. "You've said too much already, Lotta. Get out and let me handle this from here. And I've told you about those damn cigarettes," she added, sniffing the air.

Carlotta cringed, and then spoke so softly I could hardly hear her. "I'm tired of you telling me what to do, Cle. I'm twenty-two now. I can do whatever I want."

"I let you do what you want to do, and you see where it got you," said Miss Lee. "Somebody's got to take care of things. You can't. I've taken care of you the best way I can," she added, her voice strangely plaintive.

Carlotta's eyes flashed with anger. "You couldn't just let things be, could you, Cle? Why couldn't you just stay the fuck out of my life?"

"Everything I've done has been for you, and you know that as well as I do," Miss Lee said. She hovered over Carlotta, who was still sitting.

"Not me, Cle, you! From the time that I've been a kid, Cle, from the time Daddy died, it's really only been about you, about you." Carlotta was standing now, facing her aunt, her hands balled into tight little fists. "It's always about what would make things better for you, about what would give you your props.

"You gave me to that old-ass son of bitch like a present!" she continued, her voice rising. "A fucking present! What could you possibly owe him that you would give me to him like a present! What did he have on you, Cle? What kind of shit did he have on your ass?"

Miss Lee didn't look at her, and Carlotta continued, her voice getting louder with each word. "Why did you kill Gerard? What kind of deals did you all cut in the old days? What did you owe him that you had to pay?"

"I didn't kill Gerard and you know it!" Miss Lee said to Carlotta. "You as dumb as that stupid whore my brother married." A look of shame that quickly turned to rage flashed across Carlotta's face, and she slapped her aunt's face with a violent smack that nearly knocked off her wig.

"I'm sick of you talking about my mother," she muttered in a hoarse whisper. "You're nothing but a slutty old heifer who shouldn't even speak her name."

"A heifer who takes your tired, stupid behind in every time you come crawling back," Miss Lee replied with an ugly smirk, and Carlotta started tapping again, this time with her fingers on the top of the chair.

Miss Lee straightened out her wig, checking out her reflection across the room, and rubbed her hands together slowly in nervousness or anticipation. Then she backhanded Carlotta with a slap that made her reel backward from the blow and grab her cheek with a squeal, as a red streak spread like blush across her brown skin.

"I don't care what you do to me," Carlotta muttered to Miss Lee. "But I know you hated him, and I hate you because of it."

Miss Lee looked at her for a very long time and when she spoke, it was patiently and slowly. "You done said too much already. Just go on into your room," she said. Carlotta left the room without looking at me or her aunt and still touching the side of her face.

We stood there in silence for a moment, me in shock, Miss Lee rubbing the back of her hand.

"What does DeWayne have on you?"

"You think I'd tell you anything but my name?"

"Did you kill Terrence?" It occurred to me suddenly that this tiny woman with a backhand like a Riddick Bowe punch would do anything in the world she thought needed to be done—to protect herself or even her niece if driven to it.

"If I had, you think I'd be fool enough to stand up here and tell you?" Miss Lee snapped, staring at me hard as I picked up my pocketbook. And with those last words from her, I headed for the door. When I glanced back at her before I'd closed it good, her eyes were the coldest I've ever seen—on fish or human.

The clock in the Jetta, the only thing in its tired old chassis that still works like new, read three o'clock. I'd only been in there about an hour, but it had taken its toll: my head ached, my jaw was tight like I'd been doing all the yelling, and my stomach was bucking like I'd had that beer before lunch that Carlotta had drunk.

I put on some Cassandra Wilson to pull my nerves together.

The "one more day" I'd promised Jake was

drawing to a close, and I decided to go home instead of back to my office. First thing tomorrow, Tuesday morning, I'd send DeWayne his bill. By special delivery, so I'd know he got it.

I had started officially last Tuesday, a week tomorrow—and this past week had kicked my natural ass, but it was over, and soon Miss Lee, Carlotta, Gerard, Emma were names that would mean as little as they had the week before. Jake was right. Whatever surrounded them was their own mess, and had nothing to do with me and Jamal. I'd forget Basil too. As each hour passed, my passion on the kitchen floor seemed more a memory—one of those singular unforgettable moments that are only meant to happen once. Yes. Jake was right about my attraction to men who were no good for me, and it was time I did something about it.

But still I wondered. In the end, I had become as caught up in this mess as DeWayne, and it bothered me that I hadn't found any real answers.

Maybe Miss Lee had killed Terrence because she got tired of paying him to protect her niece. And exactly what *did* she have riding on Carlotta's staying with DeWayne? Or Miss Lee killed Gerard to protect Carlotta. Or maybe Carlotta had a harder edge than she'd shown me today; maybe she killed Terrence, then was forced to kill Gerard to protect herself. Or maybe Miss Lee killed them both—keeping her niece weak and dependent and making sure whatever was between her and DeWayne stayed intact? Or maybe Gerard killed Terrence, and then Miss Lee killed Gerard for good measure. Or maybe DeWayne drowned Gerard because he found Carlotta doing the do in his dead mama's house. Or maybe Emma (dare I forget her?) had done it. Hadn't she told me she hated her son? Would she be back in Daddy's good graces if *all* her ties were severed? Or maybe Basil (whom I least wanted to consider) had been tied up in this in some manner that I would never understand. Or maybe somebody who had never occurred to me had killed them both for reasons I had no idea existed. Or maybe the cops were right: Terrence had returned to his former habits and died of an overdose, just as the evidence indicated. Gerard had accidentally drowned in his grandma's tub after a last little roll with Carlotta, as all the evidence clearly said. And I, once again, had been seduced by the craziness of my former husband.

But whatever had happened, I was out of it.

And as I drove down my block, contemplating a lemon-scented bubble bath and wondering whether I should cook something for dinner or take Jamal out to Red Lobster like I'd promised last week, a grin—the first one I'd smiled in nine days—spread itself bad as it want to be across my weary lips.

14

When I thought about it later, after all that would happen was over, I cursed myself for letting my guard down, thinking things could end as easily as they had seemed to. The price for my assumption was paid in blood, and I'm not sure I'll ever forgive myself for that.

I had dreamed of Johnny the night before. He came, as he always does in my dreams, as if he had never died, dressed in that tatty red sweatsuit he used to wear, his black and tan high-top sneakers as old as sin, looking like he had when he'd bounce in after his morning run and catch me eating the chocolate donuts he always bought at Dunkin' Donuts to tempt me off my eternal diet.

I was frying potatoes and onions, heating the grease until it sizzled, and the garlic skittered across the pan. I layered the potatoes then the onions, frying them until they were soft yet crisp on the outside like my mother used to do it; I could almost taste them. I brought Johnny's plate and set it down before him, and he'd had tears in his eyes when he looked up to thank me.

"Onions make you cry, Johnny?" I'd teased him with a wink. He tilted his head with a blank, puzzled stare, and said nothing, and when I'd turned to say something else, he was gone.

I didn't think about that dream the next morning. I got up, drank myself some of my Jamaican coffee—strong with a dash of milk like I like it—popped by my office to write up DeWayne's bill and discard his computer disk, watered the orphan aloe, made a few quick calls beating the bushes for some business, and went home to catch *Oprah* for a change.

Jamal had told me he was going to be late that night. He and Hakim were hanging out, he'd said, going to play some ball in the court where they always played. They'd probably drop by McDonald's later for a burger, so I'd heated up a can of Goya black bean soup, which I like spiced up with chopped onion, a dash of hot sauce and a chopped boiled egg, and opened up a box of Triscuits.

At seven, I started listening for Jamal with the corner of my ear like mamas do. By seven-thirty, I'd rehearsed what I'd say when he finally dragged his late behind in the door. At eight, I started fidgeting—switching channels, drinking a Coke, going through my polishes so I could do my nails, all the time keeping a steady eye on that clock. And then the phone rang.

It was a woman's voice, official, gentle, and the moment I heard it, my heart stopped because I'd used that voice myself on Department business, telling somebody's mother or wife something she never wanted to hear. She told me that Hakim Curtis, my son's brother, had been shot to death a half an hour ago and that my son was an eyewitness. She asked me to come to the station to pick him up.

I'm not sure what my thoughts were then, I just knew there was raw fear that I'd never felt the likes of before pounding in the pit of my stomach. I don't know how I got there—into my car, down my street. I saw nothing—not the kids styling to the beats on the corner, not the lights I went through or drivers blowing horns calling me every name but a child of God. I turned right, left, right again, heading down Main Street to the police station. I don't remember going inside.

But I remember the tension in that room, so thick I could smell it, and the feel of grief—of mothers, fathers, wives, husbands, sisters, brothers come to claim their dead—that haunts that place, mingling like an odor with the fear and rage cops run on.

"That's the kid's mother," I heard somebody whisper.

"The dead one?"

"The other." I could feel their eyes on me—concern, pity, curiosity—and then a hush fell as a detective came forward to greet me.

He led me off the main room, into a small, separate area painted that funny shade of green that public space is painted—puke-green, somebody called it once.

Jamal sat against the wall, his body rocking to some silent song, his head hitting the back of the wall in a soft, relentless rhythm. His eyes were as empty and wide as a small scared animal's, the smell of fear still hovering. I sat down in an empty chair next to him, watched him for a moment, and then said his name. He looked at me as if he didn't know me. I grabbed him up into my arms, holding him as tightly as I could, trying to touch the pain.

I've done my share of grieving, enough for both of us, and I had irrationally hoped that my grief had somehow covered his. But I knew that night that grief can't be bartered, and it hurt me to my soul.

The cop was named Griffin. He was short for a man, about my height, but stocky, with reddish hair speckled with gray, and dark brown freckles sprinkled across caramel-colored skin. He had a reddish glow to him; they'd probably called him "Rusty" as a kid. His voice was low and soft, hushed like a priest's. He walked over to the ancient water cooler standing on the opposite side of the room, filled a thin paper cup and brought it back to Jamal.

"Here, son," he said, thrusting it toward him. Jamal took a sip and nodded a silent thank-you.

"I'm going to have to ask the boy some questions, get some kind of a statement," he said to me, looking over Jamal's head.

"It can't wait?" I asked him.

"There are things we've got to know now," he said. "Things that might change or that he might forget if we wait too long. Things he'll put out of his mind because he'll have to. It won't take long, I swear it." He pulled a chair across the room, the grating of the steel legs against the wooden floor the only sound in that small close room save the sound of Jamal breathing.

"Son," Griffin said, "we've got to talk about what happened now."

There was no light in Jamal's eyes when he looked up; he grabbed my hand, he held it like he used to when he was three. Both Griffin and I leaned forward to hear him when he finally spoke.

"He was just going to get something, something from somebody in a car," he said, shaking his head in disbelief still. Griffin and I glanced at each other in surprise and then back at him.

"Who?" I asked. "Who had something for him in a car?"

He shrugged.

"What did the person look like? What kind of car was he driving?" I was making myself talk like a cop now, think like a cop. I was tucking away that part of me that felt. *Don't feel, don't let it touch you. Think through the pain.*

"I don't know," he said, and closed his eyes, pushing against the back of the chair, straining to make himself think. "I don't know, Ma."

"Close your eyes and try to see that car. Was it a woman or a man behind the wheel?" Griffin asked, placing his hand on Jamal's shoulder as if that would make him remember. "Was it somebody he knew or you knew?"

"Take it slow, baby," I said. "Close your eyes and think, then tell us."

Jamal sighed, long and hopeless, holding my hand so tightly now it hurt. "I should have gone with him, Ma. When he ran off to the car, I should have gone with him. I could have helped him. It was dark, Ma." His words stumbled out all at once, with no connection.

He began to cry, and I glanced at Griffin asking with my eyes if we could stop. Griffin held up one finger, asking for one more minute, and Jamal spoke again, his voice barely audible.

"He said he was running late. After we finished playing, he said he was running late. I asked him what he was talking about, and he said that he had to pick up something from Daddy. That Daddy had something for him, and then he went to meet the car."

Griffin and I glanced at each other. The cop part of me could read what Griffin was thinking, and I didn't like it.

"He was meeting your father when he went to meet the car?" Griffin asked.

"Did you see DeWayne there?" I asked before Jamal could answer. "Was it your father's car?"

"No, the car was red, and Daddy's car is silver," Jamal said. "It wasn't Daddy's car. I know it wasn't Daddy. I know it wasn't Daddy's car." He looked at me, his eyes begging me to believe him. "I know the way Daddy looks in the dark. I know it wasn't Daddy."

"Tell me what he said again, as close as you can remember, son," Griffin asked.

"He just said he had to get something from Daddy. Somebody had something from Daddy, and he was late, and then he ran over to that lot where the car was parked before I could go with him, and then I heard the gun go off and the car drive away, and when I got there he was dead," Jamal said, his voice rising with each word. He began to tremble.

" 'Somebody had to give him something from Daddy.' Are you sure he said that, son?"

"Yes," Jamal said, his voice firm as if he were fully understanding it for the first time.

"He didn't say what the 'something' was?"

"No."

Griffin nodded for me to step over near the

door out of earshot of Jamal. I followed him, my eyes lingering on my son.

"Do you think his father could have had something to do with this?" he asked, watching my face closely.

"No," I said. "I don't think so. Not directly. But I think there's something else you should know. There have been other deaths. DeWayne's other sons—Gerard, Terrence—have died of unnatural causes within the last week. Another son died down south a year ago on October fourth. He was shot to death."

"Unnatural causes? What do you mean?"

"Well, the first died of a drug overdose. The second drowned accidentally in a tub."

"Within a week?" he asked, his eyes suspicious.

"Yeah."

"Where?"

"The first in Newark. The second in Belvington Heights. But the ME in both places ruled the deaths accidental."

"That was the official ruling?" He looked away, and I couldn't read what his cop's eyes were saying, eyes that wouldn't let the real story through.

"Yeah. I saw the report on Terrence."

"OK," he said, his mind considering this new piece of information and storing it. I knew the look, I'd seen it on DeLorca's face enough times. "His father is DeWayne Curtis?" he asked, with a nod toward Jamal.

"Yeah," I said. He studied Jamal and then me for a minute, something clearly on his mind. "OK, look, that's all I need now," he finally said. "I'm going to go back over to the scene, do some more checking, see if I can find any more witnesses."

He was in full cop mode now. "It could be as simple as some kid dispute we're not aware of. They all have guns now and none of them gives a damn about dying or killing somebody else. They just don't seem to know no better. He could have been mistaken for somebody else, he could have been into something neither one of us, or even your son, was aware of—" He paused for a moment, as if catching his breath or thinking of something else. "But the stuff about going to meet his father adds another angle to it, and I have to check that out." He looked at me again, as if considering whether to share something else with me; he paused a moment. "You kin to Johnny Hayle?" he finally asked.

"He was my brother."

"I was a year behind him in the Academy," he said and gave me that look—half embarrassment, half pity—that people who knew Johnny and how he died always give me. "Your brother was a good man."

"I know."

"Look, I'm going to make some calls and see if I can turn up anything else on those other deaths." His eyes surveyed me again, then warmed with reassurance. "Take him home," he added, nodding toward Jamal. "If he remembers anything else, give me a call." He pulled out a bent, slightly soiled card with his name and number on it. "Don't worry about the time." He scribbled his home number on the back. "I'll get back to you."

I'd called my doctor before I left the precinct and he prescribed a sedative for Jamal, which I picked up at an all-night drugstore on the way home and gave to him when he was ready to go to sleep. I sat on the side of his bed, we prayed together, and then I watched him go to sleep as if he were still a baby.

I glanced around his room after he was asleep, suddenly aware of the window, the closeness of our house to the street. A car backfired, and I couldn't catch my breath for a minute and a half. I slammed the window shut and pulled the shade down with a violent jerk.

Jamal's room was as messy as it always is. Clothes, socks, underwear strewn around, beneath sneakers, books and CDs, and Hakim's presence was still here, too: an old T-shirt thrown carelessly across a chair, a pile of cassettes stacked like a house of cards on the floor, videos—Double Dribble, Super Mario Bros. 2, Indy 500—lying around, and everywhere you looked, comic books with torn covers. His wide grin peeked at me from a picture of him and Jamal I'd taken at Great Adventure last year. I picked it up and held it for a moment or two, my breath catching and tears filling my eyes. *How could this shy, sweet boy be dead?*

I sat for a while longer looking around, watching Jamal, letting the grief I felt seep in, and then I went up to the attic and got a large box and filled it with red and white tissue paper. I carefully folded Hakim's clothes and stacked the other things neatly in the box, placing tissue paper between each layer. Jamal could look through these things later—maybe days, weeks or months from now. They were things he'd shared with Hakim that I knew would have meaning for him for the rest of his life.

When the doorbell rang at midnight, I knew who it was. DeWayne entered the kitchen a man defeated, shoulders slumped into themselves, his sensual lips down at the corners in a grim tight line. I'd seen him sad, that was no surprise, but he'd always managed to emerge untouched somehow—not his mother's death, or Terrence's or even Gerard's had really seemed to dim that arrogance, though that last death had made me wonder if things were coming apart for him. DeWayne was a vain man, and clothes were his measure, but even that was different tonight.

He shuffled when he walked in tonight, an old man walking an old man's gait. The expensive cashmere pullover seemed cheap and worn, the brown tweed pants that would have cost me one good day's wages fell off his body. When he sat down, neither of us spoke. He finally broke the silence.

"How many days?" he asked, more rhetorically than anything else. I didn't answer because we both knew. *Five days.* Five days between this last death and the one before it.

"I told you. Why couldn't you believe me?" he muttered accusingly, his eyes glimmering with contempt. But I cut him off, a murderous edge in my voice.

"Don't start that shit with me," I said. "I don't want to hear it tonight."

He looked away, and I followed his eyes as they settled on a Polaroid snapshot of Hakim that Jamal had taken with the camera he'd given him for his birthday last year.

"Did you talk to the cops yet?" I asked. He looked up at me like he hadn't heard me. "Did you tell somebody to give something to him, DeWayne? Jamal told the cops that he was going to meet somebody to get something for you," I continued. "Do you have any idea what he was talking about?"

"How the hell would I know something like that? Who the hell would do something like this to a kid? Who the fuck would tell that boy something like that to get at me? Tammy, *who* could hate me that much?"

"Why don't you tell me, DeWayne."

"There is nothing that I have done to anyone that would bring this on," he said, his
eyes narrowing, the anger turning suddenly
on me with an intensity that scared me. "Yeah,
I've done shit, you know I've done shit, but I
know the limits, Tamara. You know how
much people will take. I never cross the lines.
I've never done anything to bring this kind of
shit down on me."

"You've never crossed the limits with anyone? Not Miss Lee, not Basil?" I watched his
face closely looking for some revelation.

A glimmer of sadness or shame, I couldn't
tell which, crossed his face, lingering in his
eyes, but I couldn't tell what or who it was
for. Bettina? Something else, hidden from me
like that firstborn son in Salem?

He was numb with grief, there was no
doubting that, his face and eyes immobile with
sadness.

"I can't cry anymore," he said quietly.
"Tammy, I just can't cry anymore."

"Can you think of anyone—?" I didn't finish, I could see the answer in his eyes. If he
had known, then Hakim would be alive. This
was beyond his power. He was helpless, more
helpless than me.

DeWayne got up slowly and went into Jamal's room. After about fifteen minutes, I went
in and stood beside him, the years of bitterness
and contempt for each other put aside in this
moment.

Jamal was sleeping deeply, the sedative deadening him to what he had been through. DeWayne took my hand and held it, more for himself than for me. I didn't pull away.

"Can I sit here with him for a while longer, Tammy?"

"Sure."

"What if—" I knew what he was going to say. It had gone through my mind, too.

"Nothing will happen for five days, and on that day if we will protect him, take him away, keep him with us in a room just sitting with him, not letting anybody near him if we have to. We—the two of us, DeWayne—won't let anything happen to Jamal." I meant it as I said it, the words giving me strength, too. In all the times I'd known him, I'd never known that I was so much stronger. I knew that now. Another milestone had passed in my relationship with DeWayne Curtis.

"I'm going to sit here for a while," De-Wayne said. "Just a while longer."

"As long as you need to. You know where to find me if you need me."

It was two before he left. I was too wired to sleep when I went back to my bedroom, too many things were racing through my mind. In a moment of whimsy last spring, I'd painted my room bright yellow, Sunnyside Up was the color listed on the chart. I'd felt sunny and confident then, happy and sure of myself and the world. There'd been a big sale at Fortunoff's and I'd even bought a comforter sprinkled with huge daffodils to match it. But its gaiety was an insult to the memory of Hakim tonight, and I snatched it off the bed with a violent jerk. Then my own tears started so hard and fast I thought I was going to wake up Jamal. I plunged my fist in my mouth, jamming the sobs back inside me, but they kept coming, and I pulled myself into a ball to try to stifle them.

I had never wanted Jamal to know the pain that I had known when Johnny died. He knew it now, and there was nothing I could do about it. I hadn't been able to protect him from the thing I feared the most.

I stopped crying finally, exhausted and tired. I considered taking one of Jamal's pills myself. But I had to stay awake, alert, ready to act if I needed to.

Think, think, think, think, I muttered to myself, trying to calm down enough to reason, to think of what I should do.

I'd lied to DeWayne about nothing happening for five days. Whistling in the dark to a tune I didn't know. Yeah, there had been five days between Terrence and Gerard, and another five before Hakim's death, but there was no assurance that whoever was doing this would wait five days before trying to kill my son.

But even a madman has to have his reasons—a motive and an opportunity—and op-

portunity was easy enough to make if you
knew DeWayne. If you knew him, then you
knew his sons—their habits, where they lived,
how to reach them. Anyone could have shot
Hakim, anyone with half a mind to do it could
have gotten into DeWayne's mother's house to
kill Gerard. Had they checked the house for
breaking and entering? I wondered. No, probably not, knowing how that department op-
erated. Not worth the trouble. But even if they
had, this was a clever killer, I doubted that he
would leave a clue. Terrence's room was a different story. Miss Lee, Carlotta, Gerard, Basil,
maybe—through both Terrence himself and
Carlotta—they could all get to him anytime
they wanted, together or alone. Terrence and
Gerard, Gerard and Terrence, their deaths led
back to each other in a riddle of death I
couldn't solve. I was back where I started.

The key that would open this door had to
be that first death, DeWayne Jr., the one I kept
forgetting. That had been my mistake, Hakim's death had told me that. I had to get
down to Salem, Virginia, DeWayne's birth-
place where that first son had died and this
puzzle had begun.

Today was Tuesday . . . Wednesday, it was
already Wednesday morning. Then Thursday,
Friday, Saturday and finally Sunday. Sunday,
the fifth day.

There was no time. They had ruled—those
who made such decisions—that Terrence's

death was an overdose, and Gerard had drowned. It was official doctrine now, professional reputations and the dogged desire to be right were attached to those judgments.

Griffin was a good man, a good cop—I could tell that—but good cops don't jump to conclusions, they aren't sloppy, they take their time, make sure things are airtight so some smartass lawyer won't blow their game with fast-talking logic and an actor of a client that can pull a sympathetic jury's chain. Jamal would be dead if we waited for the cops to handle things.

Somebody walking over your grave. Somebody walking over your grave.

I dragged a chair from the corner of my room over to my closet, tossing down old shoe boxes (too tight), blouses (buttons missing)— every old, odd piece of clothing that good conscience should have made me send to the Goodwill and laziness kept pushing to the back of my closet. Like a crazy woman, I pushed, pulled and shoved until I finally saw it, nestled where I always knew it was, tucked way back where Jamal could never find it.

I'd packed it in a small gray combination chest with the combination taped on a piece of paper underneath it, but I didn't have to look. I remembered it even though I hadn't opened the thing in five years. I took it down now and brought it back to my bed, softly saying the combination.

I'd been on the force only six months when I'd bought my gun. They all had them, collecting them like kids collect shiny stones, and I wanted my own "toy" too—a .38 Smith & Wesson, Model 64, stainless steel, which shimmered like silver when I opened the chest tonight.

Johnny's gun had killed him. If he hadn't had one ready and loaded, he'd be alive today. One had killed Hakim tonight. But the power of the gun is seductive, the power to take life, the power to protect. I held the gun, repulsed yet fascinated, contemplating the death it always brings. No good can ever come of guns, I know that like I know my name, but I loaded it now quickly without a second thought. And I knew at that moment that whoever dared to hurt my son would have to come through me first. I would die to save Jamal's life, and take anyone with me who tried to touch him.

15

It was Thursday night. Every hour brought Sunday closer. We had gathered at DeWayne's big Tudor on Keer Avenue across from Weequahic Park a few hours after the service for Hakim. Hakim's mother had become a Muslim a few days after his birth, and his grandma had buried her grandson in that tradition the day after his death.

I'd never been to DeWayne's house before, and the moment I stepped in I recognized things that had come and gone with him when we'd been together—his mama's antique clock, a teal blue pitcher he'd won in a raffle, the bright pink shag rug we'd picked out together that had been on our bedroom floor the night I'd stalked out. His living room had a thrown-together look about it—red crushed-velvet couch sitting on my bright pink shag sitting on pale blue carpeting—as if each of his wives had left some discarded bit of herself,

217

which he'd thrown together in a mishmash of clashing styles, hues and textures. He'd always been a pack rat, and his bad taste had survived four marriages.

Jamal and DeWayne sat together in a far corner of the room. Miss Lee, who had been here when Jamal and I walked in, sat in an orange wing chair, her narrow eyes lighting on each of the assembled guests and finally coming to rest on DeWayne and my son.

July, in a white suit flitting in and out of the kitchen like a butterfly on bennies, helped gathered neighbors lay out food on the large dining room table covered with a holly and wreath tablecloth. I sat on the velvet couch sipping cheap Chablis on ice from a Jurassic Park glass compliments of McDonald's.

I had slept badly the night before, dreams of Johnny haunting me. I'd awakened with a start at seven and started calling airlines to make reservations for Friday morning on the earliest thing smoking to Roanoke, Virginia, the closest I could get by public transportation to Salem. I booked a 6:40 A.M. Northeast Express leaving Friday morning that would get me into Roanoke by 8:40, and made reservations back to Newark on Saturday night at 5:28.

I wasn't sure what I was looking for in Salem, but I figured I'd start by talking with the boy who was in jail for killing DeWayne Jr., and then check out Willa, DeWayne Jr.'s mother, and then see what the cops would be willing to share. Everything was a long shot: getting to see the kid, talking to Willa, all in less than two days' time, but if I could find out anything that tied with what was happening up here, it would be worth it. Whatever I did, it would have to be fast. I took a sip of wine and saw DeWayne talking to Jamal; they were both oblivious of Miss Lee, who watched them like a hawk.

Was that hate in her eyes?

"What do you have on Cleotha Lee?" I'd asked DeWayne when he'd called me this morning to tell me about the arrangements for Hakim.

"Did she say I had something on her? I've told you all I know. I haven't done a damn thing worth any bitch or son of a bitch killing my sons over."

"You must have or they wouldn't be dying."

"If I knew, don't you think I would tell you?" His voice broke then in a way that told me that there was no sense in pushing it. Whatever it was, he didn't remember it or had sealed it so tight within him he would never let it go for anybody's life but his own. He'd asked if I wanted Jamal to stay with him, and I'd snapped that there was only one person I could trust to keep my son, who I knew would give his life to protect him. He didn't ask me who it was, and I didn't tell him. But I had asked for information and he'd given it: Willa's number and the name of the cop, Jenkins, who was in charge of DeWayne Jr.'s case.

Then I called Jake, and Phyllis had answered. I'd felt a twinge of guilt as I always did whenever I spoke to her, even though Jake and I have never done anything worth being ashamed of and never will as long as they are together.

She told me that Jake would be out until late that afternoon, so I told her what I would have told Jake and prayed that she was lucid enough to understand what I was saying. Sometimes she was as she had always been: "normal" with a drop-dead sense of humor. But other times she could be like a ghost, and sometimes there was the demon—a shrill, sarcastic bitch who made you wonder why you had never sensed that part of her before. On a demon day, she would "forget" things just for spite.

She seemed OK this morning, sweetly repeating what I'd told her—that Hakim had died, that I was going out of town, that I wanted Jamal to stay with them till I got back on Saturday night, for Jake to meet me at DeWayne's. She spoke slowly and deliberately like a not-too-bright kid repeating a lesson she'd learned by heart.

"Tamara?" she'd asked, *Tam-ah-rah*, saying each syllable of my name in that dramatic, pretentious style she sometimes affected.

"Yeah, Phyl," I said, talking to her like I had when we'd been girls.

"Jake will keep Jamal safe, don't worry." She said it with a certainty that brought tears to my eyes.

"I know, Phyl. I know," and my voice caught as I remembered again that she believed in him as much as I did. "Don't forget to tell Jake what I said, and don't tell anybody else. Nobody else, OK?" I added cautiously.

"OK," she said slowly. I had her write down DeWayne's address and telephone number, and she hung up, me praying that she would remember.

I'd tried calling him again later on that morning, but nobody was home, and I'd tried again before I'd left the house. I didn't know what I would do with Jamal if Jake didn't show up.

"How about something to eat?" July asked, snapping me from my thoughts with a plate full of greens, potato salad and fried chicken—comfort food, Southern-style.

"Girl, you didn't have to bring this over," I said, picking up the chicken leg and stuffing the thigh into my mouth. Until July had given me the plate, I hadn't realized how hungry I was. I picked up a forkful of potato salad, dropping a slice of potato heavy with mayonnaise on my lap in the rush to my mouth. With no shame, I picked it up and shoved it back into my mouth.

"Hey, this last one has left everybody stunned," she said, sitting down next to me. "I just want to do everything I can. But, damn, I'm tired," she said with an exaggerated swipe at her brow.

"Yeah, you've definitely been working your butt off. I hope DeWayne knows how lucky he is," I said, taking a sip of wine.

"He won't know the half of it till I'm gone," she said, with a little chuckle. "That's what I need," she said, pointing to my wine. "Save my spot." She got up and came back with a glass filled with liquor. "Bourbon," she said with a nod at the glass. "That's my drink. Bourbon." She took a long slow swallow and then a quick sip like an afterthought. "That's more like it. Bourbon."

"My brother used to drink bourbon."

"Really?" She glanced at me, a shadow of a thought passed over her eyes, and I figured she was remembering our last talk, the one about Johnny and her mother.

"You think a lot about your brother, huh?"

"Yeah," I said. "Every day. It doesn't get any easier."

"Nobody knows that any better than me. Death does have a way of kicking your natural ass," she said philosophically, in what I'd begun to realize was her typically blunt manner. "No matter how long somebody's been gone, if that person was all you had, that's all you can think about."

222

We both looked over toward DeWayne and Jamal.

"Are you going to let your son stay with his father?"

"Why would I do that?"

"Because he's down to one." She shrugged. "I guess because of all that's happened, I thought he might want him to stay with him sometime."

"He's staying with me," I said more forcefully than I meant it to sound.

"You know he and Carlotta broke up."

"I heard."

"You think they'll get back together? He's having such bad luck with sons, maybe he'll decide it's time to try again."

"What the hell is wrong with you, July?" I snapped.

"What?"

"Why do you say such stupid, thoughtless shit all the time?" My nerves were plucked, and I was too raw to be polite or even give a damn.

"I don't know," she said thoughtfully, taking a sip of bourbon. The look on her face pointed to a sadness I sensed she wasn't ready to share. But I'd been there too, hadn't I? "I'm sorry," she said, glancing up at me. "I think it's one of the ways I have of dealing with grief, with things that go so deep I don't want to feel them. I trivialize shit all the time, Tamara. Then it can't hurt me. There's a lot of things about myself I don't understand."

"Welcome to the club."

"It just comes out, you know, the stuff I'm always saying, the way shit always does. I guess I'm too honest, you know? But, I'm sorry," she said. "I'm really sorry."

"No big thing," I said with a shrug, taking another sip of wine. *Who the hell was I to judge?* I thought to myself. "I'm sorry. I didn't mean to snap. My nerves are shot."

"Still friends?" she asked like a little girl.

"Yeah," I said. "I need every friend I can get." We both laughed, and she gave me a girlfriend hug.

Miss Lee got up and walked to the table, took a plate and filled it high with food. She walked back past DeWayne, stooping to whisper something to him, and then returned to her place. She glanced over at us, her face as hard as a rock.

"I don't think that lady likes me," July said.

"That look was for me, not you," I said. "We had some words on Monday, and she's obviously still pissed."

"I don't know what her thing is with DeWayne," July said offhandedly. "At first I figured it was just Carlotta, but now I'm not so sure."

"That makes two of us. Does she ever show up at Branford Place?"

"Every now and then."

"They go back. I think I met her before,

when DeWayne and I were married. There are things about my ex-husband I don't know and they're beginning to fuck with me on a daily basis. I never know when some shitty little thing he's forgotten to tell me is going to pop up and smack me across the face," I added, momentarily confidential, a way I'm not prone to be, but my guard was down due, I guess, to the general turn our conversation had taken and the wine I was steadily sipping.

I don't like to get drunk, a nice mellow buzz is as far as I'll take things, and I knew I was probably drinking more than I should tonight. Things had gotten to that point. *What if I couldn't find any answers? What if there were no answers to get? Finding my peace in the bottom of a bottle.* My mother used to talk about my father like that. He'd been a happy drunk, and what I hadn't told July about Johnny and his favorite drink was that Johnny drank more bourbon sometimes than he probably should have. He'd been drunk the night he'd done it; I was sure of that.

July chuckled. "Sounds like you got a problem," she said, startling me, until I realized she wasn't reading my mind but commenting on DeWayne.

"Yeah," I said, smiling half at myself for getting lost in my own thoughts. "Sounds like I do."

The doorbell rang, and Carlotta Lee Curtis,

surprising the hell out of everybody, switched into the room.

"Well," July purred nastily. "Look what the cat done drug in."

Carlotta seemed to have recovered from our meeting on Monday, but not completely. Shades of grief still hovered around the edges. Her dress was a navy wool number, which fit her loosely, almost matronly. She wore little makeup and no jewelry at all this time. Every time I saw this chick she looked like somebody else.

DeWayne perked up like a guard dog when she walked in, but then his face dissolved into an expression somewhere between annoyance and surprise. He rose in his chair as if to stand in protest as she approached him, and then dropped back down, resigned. Jamal watched her as she walked toward them, studying her every movement as carefully as if she were a wolf and he were a rabbit. I knew he remembered how she had treated Hakim, and his face showed those memories more clearly than any words he could have uttered. I stood up protectively to go to him, but he rose suddenly with neither a word nor glance at DeWayne or Carlotta and came over to where July and I were sitting. Carlotta squeezed into the space that he'd left and began to talk quietly to DeWayne, intimately, as if nothing had changed between them.

Jamal slumped down on the couch beside

me. "I hate her," he muttered quietly. "I hate her."

"You don't hate anyone, son," I said more from convention than conviction, and Jamal threw me a look that told me he thought I was full of crap.

"I hate her because she hated Hakim," he said quietly.

"Well . . ." I started, trying to sound adult, "I don't think Carlotta really hated Hakim, but—"

"I'm inclined to agree with the boy," July said.

"Don't make things worse," I snapped.

"Why are you defending her?" Jamal asked me sharply. "How could you say that when you know what Hakim used to say about her? You know how she felt about him." He was talking loudly now and several people glanced up, including DeWayne.

I put my arm around Jamal, staring everyone down.

"I want to go home," he said, sounding like a spoiled kid. "What are we waiting for? I want to go home."

"I want to wait a few more minutes," I said. We were waiting for Jake, but I didn't want to say that. I hadn't told him about my plans or that he was staying with Jake until Saturday night. I didn't want him to worry, and I didn't want him mentioning it to the wrong person. "Just try to cool out for a few more minutes."

At that moment, the doorbell rang, and Jake came in. Our eyes locked, and then we glanced away from each other like we always did in public. I knew that he had come to see me, but he had too much class to make that his obvious, immediate goal in the middle of a gathering like this. He walked over to Hakim's grandmother and took her hand, holding it for a moment and whispering to her softly, and then he went over to DeWayne.

"We can go home in a couple of minutes," I whispered to Jamal, who got up and stalked into the rec room where DeWayne kept the TV and the VCR.

"Things are getting to your boy," July said with concern. "But, ummmph, uumph, huumph, who is that who just came in," she added in the same breath in a lusty, throaty whisper as soon as Jamal was out of earshot. She gestured toward Jake, keeping her eyes on him like he was a piece of that chicken she'd just brought me.

"He's married," I said quickly.

"Not too, I hope."

I shot her a look, and she backed off with a playful shrug. I changed my expression, embarrassed by my reaction. But my feelings about Jake—the strange mix of emotions that I've tried to keep control over for longer than I care to admit—were too obvious to hide, and I was too tired and high to try.

"Sorry," she said. "Didn't mean to step on somebody's toes."

"Nobody's toes were stepped on."

She gave me a coy, know-it-all look. "But he is one good-looking bastard. What's his name?"

"Jake."

"Jake. Sounds like rake. He looks kind of rakish with that fine broad back, and that nice tight ass. He looks like he works out."

"I couldn't tell you," I said with annoyance. Jake caught my eye and gave me a nod toward the kitchen, telling me to meet him in there if I got a chance, but July saw it.

"If you don't go, I will. Opportunity doesn't knock on this rusty old door too often, and when it does I'm definitely ready to open it wide." She chuckled lecherously. I knew she didn't mean anything by it, but it annoyed the hell out of me anyway.

"No, seriously," she continued. "If you're not interested in pursuing something like that, I am. I believe in going for what I want."

"I don't chase married men," I said sanctimoniously, then regretted the Goody Two-Shoes sound of my voice. *I've got to cut this shit out*, I thought, but even as I scolded myself I realized that there was more to my reaction than just my feelings about Jake. It was July's eyes. The hunger in them. Hunger, desperation and fear. The fear of her own loneliness and her own vulnerability. Fear that every woman, including me, feels more times than she wants to own up to. *Was it myself that I was seeing? Was that why she was annoying me?* I took another sip of wine.

"You got a lot weighing on you, girlfriend," she said, her tone light and patronizing. Jake came over to where we were sitting, and July stood up, extended her hand, introducing herself with a big smile.

"Are you a friend of Tamara's? I'm July, a friend too," she said as she pushed her way toward him, so close it was embarrassing. I caught the puzzled look in his eye, but he was too polite to say anything.

July noticed it too and moved back to give him some space. "On my way," she said. "Some girls have all the luck."

"She says what's on her mind," Jake said to me as soon as she was out of earshot. "Acts it too. You OK?"

"Yeah."

"So who is she?"

"You sound like you're interested. De-Wayne's secretary."

"I see the rest of the gang is here too," he said, looking around. "Cleotha Lee, right?" He nodded toward Miss Lee.

"Yeah, you were definitely right on that one." So much had happened since I'd talked to him Sunday night, I didn't have the strength or will to explain it.

"So do you know who if anyone told

DeWayne about Carlotta and his late son?"

"He found out, they broke up, and now . . .
your guess is as good as mine," I said, nodding toward DeWayne and Carlotta sitting together on the couch.

"You never know what's really going on
with somebody or how it's going to mess with
you eventually," Jake said, sounding philo-
sophical. I looked him over for a minute and
a half knowing that he was right and wondered if there was any shit about him I didn't
know, and deciding that there was.

"Is she part of the reason you're going down
to Virginia?" he asked, nodding toward Miss
Lee.

"Yeah. I think there are secrets between her
and DeWayne. Serious secrets."

"How do you know you're going to find
anything down there, or anywhere? Do you
think maybe you should let the professionals
handle it, Tam?" he asked.

"I *am* a professional, Jake."

"Sorry, Tam," Jake said quickly. "But you're
dealing with somebody who will pop a sixteen-year-old kid without blinking twice.
Somebody who's crazy enough to kill two
young men in a way that makes no sense except to him. You're dealing with somebody
who is out of his mind, Tam. Are you sure
you're ready for this?"

"I can't just sit on my ass and wait. I've got
to do something. Should I wait for a cop, Jake?

Give me a break. I am more afraid than I've ever been of anything in my life. I have to do something."

"Don't let Jamal know that you're as scared as you are."

"I'm scared shitless, and he knows it. Even if I wanted to fool him I couldn't." I took a break. "So you'll be able to watch him?"

"No problem."

"You're always there for me."

Jake shrugged my comment off like he always does when I thank him for a favor.

"You know what you and Jamal mean to me," he said quietly. "I'm taking Phyllis and the kid down to see her mother in Camden on Friday night; we'll just take him with us. Phyllis said you'll be back in town Saturday night, right? I'll drive Jamal back then, get you at the airport, then drive back down to Camden and pick them up. Unless you want me to stick around? Do you need me here?"

I thought about it for a minute, wondering if I did. "That's OK," I finally said. "I got this cop Griffin's home number so I'll call him when I get back and tell him anything I find. He can tell me what to do about Sunday. The plane gets in at eight forty-nine. So Phyllis told you everything? She really seemed OK."

"You know better than that," Jake said without a trace of bitterness. He glanced away and changed the subject.

232

"What are you going to do when you get down there?"

"Talk to people. It's a small town. He told me that much about it when we were married. Small and gossipy, everybody minding everybody else's business. DeWayne called down there and told his son's mother and the cop who was handling the case I was coming. Maybe it's not Miss Lee," I said, more to myself than to Jake now. "Maybe it's somebody else who knows her or Carlotta or has something on him that DeWayne doesn't know. I don't know what I'll find down there, Jake, except I have to go; I can't think of anything else to do."

We both sat there, not saying anything for a minute, me wondering how Jamal would react when I told him I was leaving town and feeling how good Jake's strong, firm leg felt leaning into mine.

"You ready to go home now?"

"Yeah," I said.

"Why don't we play it this way," he said, speaking softly, his eyes surveying the room. "Why don't you get up in a couple of minutes. I'll walk you to the car. I'll come back in, hang out for a while and then drive by to get Jamal about midnight. That will give you time to pack some stuff for him and explain what's going on. You didn't say anything to him yet, did you?"

"No, I didn't. It's probably somebody in this

room, huh?" I asked, my eyes following his, watching each face for some sign, some give-away twitch or weird sneer that would tell me what I wanted to know.

"What do you think?"

"I don't know. What about Basil?" I asked very quickly, not wanting him to hear the anx-iousness.

"What about him?" Jake studied me closely.

"Do you think it could be him?"

"You know him better than me."

I knew he was right, that my eyes or the turn of my mouth probably gave me away every time he mentioned Basil's name, and there was nothing I could do to change that. Jake had always been able to read people, es-pecially me, in ways that half the time made me swear he was clairvoyant and the other half made me think he was having me tailed. Trying to fool or lie to him was as useless as spitting in the wind.

July came back and set her drink down on the table in front of us.

"Mind if I leave this here?" she asked. We stopped talking, and Jake smiled up at her.

"Why don't you sit down?" he said, getting up. "Did you say you were ready to go, Ta-mara? I don't mind walking you to your car," he said formally to me.

"Thanks, Jake. I'll see you later, July. It was good talking to you."

"Nice meeting you," she said to Jake. "I'm sure our paths will cross again."

I went to fetch Jamal, who was sitting in front of the TV set in the den watching Ren and Stimpy on Nickelodeon, and mouthing "Happy, happy, joy, joy" like his life depended on it.

"Jamal," I said gently, touching his arm. He looked up. "Come on, it's time to go."

"Is *she* still with Daddy?"

"Yeah."

He didn't say anything. When he came back into the living room he watched Carlotta suspiciously, staring at her evenly.

As always happens when one person gets up to go, everybody else got up too, almost on cue. The three of us were silent as we walked slightly behind the others to our car, but Jake put his arm protectively around Jamal's shoulder.

I didn't tell Jamal I was going to Virginia and why I was going until we got home. He didn't say too much about it. I figured he was numb and just as dead tired as I was. Jake came by about midnight to pick him up and gave me the number of Phyllis's mother in Camden where they would be staying Friday night. When I walked Jamal to the door, he started crying again but he tried to hide it in front of Jake. Jake gave him that kind of half-hug, half-grab men comfort each other with to let him know it was OK to cry. As we left the house, I looked around the block, making sure nobody else was around. I watched Jamal climb into the back seat and lie down like he used to when he was five, and then I watched the car pull away and I stood there until it had turned the corner.

I packed quickly after they'd gone, took a shower so I wouldn't have to do it in the morning and set my clock for 5:30 A.M. Then I climbed into bed and lay there thinking about Hakim and his death. *The red car. Who had it belonged to?* A thought came suddenly that chilled me, then without thinking twice about it or even assuming I'd get an honest answer if I asked, I picked up the phone and dialed.

"Yeah," he answered.

"It's Tamara."

"Hey." His voice was soft and husky as if he were just waking up or drifting off to sleep, and a physical thrill that I tried to squelch went through my body. "I'm glad you called. You in bed?"

"Basil, what color is your car?"

He paused for a moment, as if he weren't sure what to make of the question, and then he sighed as if he was suddenly very tired or very bored. "Any color you want it to be, baby. Any color you want it to be," he said and hung up.

I lay back on the bed then and pulled the covers up around my neck, staring at the ceiling, doubts about him, my choices in men, the red car, and my own judgment keeping me awake. I finally drifted off to sleep around three-thirty, two hours before I had to get up.

16

My grandma used to say no matter how fast you run, your past is sure to grab you. Grandma's face was thin and angular, like one of those Ife masks you see hanging in a museum. She used to plait my hair and tie it tight with red ribbons that hung down my back like streamers. She died when I was ten, right after the riots, around the time we left Newark. Ever since this whole mess started, my dead had been calling me. I was down here chasing ghosts, and they were starting to chase me back.

I'd gotten into Roanoke, Virginia, on Friday morning, checked into a Comfort Inn and made two calls: one to Willa Johnson, De-Wayne Jr.'s mama, and the other to Jenkins, the cop who was handling the case against the kid they said killed her son. I couldn't see the kid, Darnell Lewis, without going through his lawyer. But he wasn't going anywhere because he didn't have the money for bail. He had more time than I did. Jenkins, a soft-spoken blond with a wide-eyed, country-boy manner too sweet for a cop, told me that the kid was there because of circumstantial evidence— driving the dead man's car, buying a watch with his credit card—dumb kid shit, pure and simple. But he was sporting a juvey record, which made him a particularly attractive suspect. He swore he hadn't done it.

I'd gone to bed that night dead tired and discouraged, wondering if I should have left Jersey, thinking about Basil, hoping that seeing Willa Johnson would make the trip down here worth the money and time. In the spirit of the pessimist that I tend to be, I was prepared to be disappointed as I walked up the path to her small, woodframe house.

At 44, Willa Johnson was two years younger than DeWayne, a soft-talking woman with a broad, generous body and delicate beauty that had probably faded by the time she'd had her second kid. She looked her age if not a few years older, but she was relaxing into middle age with that comfortable acceptance that marks women genuinely satisfied with their lot in life. I recalled with annoyance how DeWayne had brushed her off that first time he'd mentioned his son, not even saying her name until I'd asked for it. But by the looks of her and the small, neat house and peaceful vibe, she'd had the last laugh.

With a wide smile she welcomed me into her kitchen, which smelled vaguely of cinnamon and lemon Joy, and within fifteen minutes we were sharing intimacies, courtesy of our common bond: DeWayne Curtis. I told her what had happened to DeWayne's sons, what the cops said, what we knew, and that I was afraid for the life of *my* son. She listened sympathetically, held my hand for a moment. When her eyes clouded over, I knew she was remembering her own dead boy.

"He was my firstborn," she said after a few minutes. "This year has been one of the hardest of my life, Tamara, one of the hardest of my life. I have the others, but one child can never replace another.

"Somehow I know that boy they're holding, Darnell whatever his name is, didn't kill my boy. They sewed it up so neat, so easy, those cops did, but it didn't seem to make no sense." We sat there in silence for a moment, and then she looked up at me and gave me a sad half-smile.

"Want something to eat?" she asked quickly. "I'm going to make myself a sandwich, want one?" Black women and food, sisterly comfort when you need it—brothers may fail you, money may fly, but there's always good food and the grace to offer it. I thought about July and how she'd brought me over that plate of chicken and potato salad the night before last at DeWayne's house.

"Yes, thanks," I said. I *was* hungry, that was for sure. I'd meant to get by to see her earlier, but I'd gone over to the station trying to see the kid again, without any luck. It was 2:15 now, way past my lunchtime.

She opened the refrigerator and took out a bag of bread, some baloney and a large jar of mayonnaise, which she spread thick on four slices of bread and then slapped four slices of baloney down on each one.

"Here you go." She handed a plate to me, sat down opposite and took a bite. "I haven't thought a lot about him through these years. DeWayne Senior, I mean. I had the boy, my son DeWayne Junior. But I didn't think a lot about his daddy. I had the others, you know." She gestured toward a dated, slightly greasy Polaroid tacked up on the wall above the stove of three young children, probably teen-agers by now. "Joy, Linda, Audrey. I married their daddy, Henry, after DeWayne and I broke up, right after DeWayne Junior was born."

"What was he like when you knew him? DeWayne Senior, I mean."

She watched me for a moment, and then smiled as if remembering. "He was a very sweet boy when I knew him. I guess he wasn't really a boy though, was he? DeWayne was twenty-two when DeWayne Junior was born. I was twenty. Young, wasn't I? Nothing but a young girl."

"Did he have family? People he was close to?"

"His mother and father were divorced, which was *something* for those times. Nobody got divorced then, you just lived through the meanness. But DeWayne's parents had done it. Made him kind of special to us kids. He stayed with his aunt, who was much older, and his cousins. He was close to his older cousin, Delroy, who was much older than DeWayne, kind of between an older brother and a young father."

"DeWayne said he knew a woman named Cleotha Lee when he lived down here. Do you remember her?"

"Cleotha Lee? Lord, I haven't heard that name in years! Girl, you sure are down here stirring up some memories. She used to go with Delroy. Oooh, girl, that takes me back. Way before DeWayne and me."

"There are some people who think she could be the person who is doing the killing," I said, lying for no other reason than it sounded good. The truth was *nobody* thought it but me. "She's the only person who has ties to him down here, and this is where things could have started."

"Cleotha used to go with Delroy. But she hasn't been down here in years. I don't think she could have had anything to do with my son's death."

"Does she have family down here?"

"She had a brother, and somebody said he had a child, she left to be with him and the woman he married, who people said wasn't no good, but I don't know much about them. What makes you think Cleotha would have anything to do with DeWayne Junior's death? There wouldn't be any reason for her to hurt him."

"That's what I'm down here to find out," I said. "What happened between them?"

She took a small, dainty nibble off her sandwich and then put it back on her plate, dabbing the corner of her mouth with one of the folded paper towels that she had put out for us in lieu of napkins. "Nothing happened between DeWayne and Cleotha. Anything happened, it happened between her and Delroy. They were getting married. But then he broke it off. She had a child. His child. The baby died. DeWayne and those dead babies," she said, as if this thought unrelated to anything else had just floated into her mind. "I've never known a man who seemed to have so much of his life tied up with dead babies, even now," she added in amazement as if was an afterthought.

"Dead babies? How did Cleotha's baby die?"

"You know you can't put much stock in what people say, and I don't like to repeat tales from folks who half the time don't know what the heck they're talking about. But there was talk when she left."

"What kind of talk?"

"This was a long time ago. When me and DeWayne were kids. You know you hear talk from grown people, half-whispered stuff before you come into a room. You only half-hear mess when you're a kid."

"How did the baby die?"

"They say she killed it. She didn't want it. Everybody knew she always had a mean streak, Cleotha did. We were all half scared of her when we were little. Even DeWayne, he was about eleven then, I was nine."

I tried to imagine the DeWayne that I knew now with the open grinning face of youth. And Cleotha Lee—how had she looked? Willa glanced at me and continued.

"People said, those who were doing the talking, that she smothered it while it slept. But I think that baby died of crib death. That's all, but they didn't know nothing about no crib death back then. They used to say if a baby died like that, that the cat got his breath, or his mama rolled over on him, or some evil somebody smothered him, or something like that. Cleotha's baby probably died natural, but you know how folks talk. Here she was back then, a young girl with a baby, and it dies, and she's known to be as mean as a wet cat in heat. You know how people talk."

Had Cleotha *ever* been a frightened young

woman? Scared she'd killed her baby or that people thought she did? Maybe that was what had turned her into who she'd become. Or maybe not.

"So what did DeWayne have to do with that?" I asked, bringing it back to DeWayne again and the reason I was down here.

"He was living there when it happened. He was staying with them. But he wasn't nothing but a boy. He didn't have nothing to do with it. Nothing at all."

A sinking feeling of profound disappointment came over me. I'd come all the way down here, looking for some tie, some connection between Cleotha Lee and DeWayne, and this was it? I'd come for this? I tried one last, desperate stab.

"Do you think it's possible that Cleotha Lee could have killed the baby, and DeWayne saw it and has blackmailed her for all these years?" It sounded foolish to me even as I said it.

Willa Johnson looked at me for a moment, puzzled, and then shook her head sadly. "Baby," she said gently with pity, "I know you came down here like you said—to save your boy, to find out what you could—and I wish I could help you, but DeWayne was eleven or twelve years old when this thing happened. He stayed with them, with Cleotha and Delroy, on and off, but Cleotha didn't kill that baby, and if she had, he couldn't have known nothing about it. He was a boy himself, doing things boys do—cutting class, chasing girls, stealing apples off white folks' trees. And he was such a sweet boy, DeWayne was. A sweet, gentle boy, good-hearted. It would never occur to a boy like that to blackmail somebody."

"A sweet, gentle boy, good-hearted," I repeated more in disbelief than mockery.

"Yes," she said.

"But there has to be something else," I said desperately, like a kid not wanting to leave Great Adventure. Suddenly I felt like a fool. What could I have been thinking? Jake's words came back: "Let the professionals handle it." I was down here chasing ghosts when I should have gotten my son and gone to stay with my sister, Pet, done something sensible. No, I had to be the big-time detective. Make some money. End up putting the only person who meant anything to me in danger. A thought followed by a sense of dread swept me. *Basil. He was who was left. Were things leading back to Basil Dupre, who knew where I lived, who knew what my boy looked like, who knew where Hakim and he played ball; who'd played me like a class-A fool?* My sandwich felt so dry in my mouth I couldn't swallow.

"But I remember that boy's sadness, DeWayne's sadness, when that baby died," Willa continued with a sigh, unaware of the look in my eyes and that my throat felt like it was closing. "You finished?" she asked, glancing at my half-eaten sandwich. I looked up at her.

"You OK, honey?"

"Yeah, fine," I said.

"You look kind of peaked."

"I'm okay," I said, but my thoughts were in Jersey: on Basil, on Jamal. She cleared my dish, putting both our plates in the sink and turning on the faucet full force.

"Maybe that was what attracted me to him so much later, remembering what a sweet boy he was and how he'd mourned. Cleotha's child when he was a boy, and Willow's boy later. It seemed like DeWayne had more sadness than any one man had a right to have," she said, reminiscing. She sat back down, and glanced up at the clock. It read two forty-five.

"Willow's boy? Who was Willow?" I asked, more out of politeness than anything else.

Willa put the mayonnaise jar and the bread back in the refrigerator, then took a sponge and wiped the spot in front of us where our plates had been. "Willow was the girl who DeWayne was with before he came to me. Willow. I used to tease him, tell him that he liked me because my name was so much like hers, Willa, Willow. I'd never heard that name before, except for a tree. It's a pretty name, though, isn't it? Now that was one sad, sad story." She sat back down shaking her head. "I wish I could be more helpful. I wish I could tell you something. But I don't think Cleotha

Lee would kill those boys, there would be no reason for her to do it."

"What happened to Willow?"

"She died. Killed herself."

My breath caught the way it always did whenever anyone said those words, my own loss coming up again. *Would it never leave me, the way Johnny died?*

"That almost destroyed that boy. I think that's why I fell in love with him so quickly, why I had our baby, DeWayne Junior, as quickly as I did, trying to heal his pain in the only way a twenty-year-old country girl knows how: with my body, giving him a baby to replace the one he'd lost. He loved that child so, that baby son. He never talked about it afterward. It was like he blocked it out, just blocked out that whole three years they were together, Willow, Willow's little girl, the baby they had. It was such a tragedy. But he was just a boy when they were together. I think he got his manhood with her, with Willow."

"Her suicide destroyed DeWayne?" I asked, and my anger at him followed the familiar path straight to my gut. *How could he not have told me of his loss, knowing about mine?*

"Yes, that and more, I think, the death of their baby boy. Terrell, I think his name was. He wasn't more than three months old when he died."

"How did it happen? Was that a crib death too?"

"No. There was no doubt about what happened there. An accident. DeWayne was watching the children, and the little girl, Willow's little girl, dropped that baby on his head, and he died. DeWayne's son, his firstborn. He never said it, but I could read it in his eyes. He always blamed himself."

Nothing. In all the time I'd known him.

"He never told me anything about it," I said quietly, the weight of what she'd just told me making it hard to talk.

"I think it changed him in ways that we can't even know," said Willa softly. "I think it killed some part of him. He changed within that year we were together. I loved one man, part of that sweet boy I'd known, and he changed into somebody else, right while I was watching—mean-spirited, short with me, secretive. He left me and our son, went to New York, yeah, he sent me money sometimes, every month what he could spare. But today I wouldn't know him if he walked into this room."

"What happened to the little girl?" I asked. "The little girl who dropped the baby."

"Willow? That was her name. Her mama named her after herself. That's one thing I would never do, name a baby girl after me, even though I guess Willa is as good a name as any. It gives a child so much to bear. You never know what life will serve you, or what you're putting on a child. In Willow's case it was quite a bit, seeing she died like that, taking her own life and all.

"I don't rightly know what happened to little Willow. Her mama and DeWayne were common-law, she was a couple of years older than he was, so he had no right to keep her daughter, and Willow's people were poor. Somebody said they sent her to live with some of their people, down deep south, though I heard that her people weren't all that right in the head. That's where they sent the child, I reckon. I guess she went to family. Such a shame, the way it happened. The whole town talked about it, a little girl killing her baby brother like that. Baby born in July, dead by October."

I don't know why my mind made the connection, maybe hearing the two months said so close like that: July. October. July.

"*Miss July.*"

"*No, July is my first name.*"

"*You were born in July?*"

"*No, October. My mama had a sense of humor.*"

Born in July and dead by October. A mother dead by her own hand? *July was Willow's child.* A chill went through me, so deep and strong, straight to my bones, and I shivered despite the glow of the sun that beamed into the kitchen. It was a chill that told me I was right.

"Do you remember what day of the month the baby died?" I asked Willa. I knew she didn't. I did, though, I was sure of it. *The fourth*

*day of October. The day of her son's death a year
ago. The day when Terrence died.*

Willa looked at me blankly, seeing the terror
in my eyes.

"How old was the little girl?" I asked.

"Willow's daughter? About five or six."

The age was right. Maybe the history too.
My bones told me it was.

There had to have been a death notice,
something about the death, human interest,
talk of tragedy.

"How long after the baby died did the
mother die?"

"Shortly after? A couple of days. Shot herself through the head. How could a mother
shoot herself through the head so her daughter
would find her? Maybe she was crazy, crazy
from the grief."

The local newspaper had to have done
something, I thought, my thoughts coming
fast now. There had to be a photograph of Willow, of her daughter, I needed something that
would tell me I was right. I stood up quickly,
and Willa stood up with me, watching me cautiously, not sure what to make of me.

"Is there a library in town? Somewhere they
keep old newspaper stories in files, on microfiche?"

"Salem Public Library," she said. "Let me
write down how to get there." But I was out
the door before she could find a pencil.

17

A kid pointed me toward the Salem Public Library, and in about fifteen minues I was walking through the door. The place looked the way all small-town libraries look on a Saturday afternoon: weary young mamas hauling toddlers to the picture-book corner, late-ass high schoolers cramming for that exam they should have studied for last week, old dudes leafing through the sports pages—a low-key crowd with nowhere better to go. I usually like libraries, they calm me down, make me feel earnest and worthy; the pale walls and hushed silence bring out the intellectual in me. But not today.

My hands were shaking as I wrote down the dates on the request sheet for the issues of the paper I needed. The research librarian, a cheerful, plump brunette in her late thirties with a soft Southern accent that matched her slow-as-molasses smile, could probably read the anxiety in my face. She got me the microfiche for the local weekly paper and threaded it into the microfiche machine fast, as though my life depended upon it. I wasn't sure it didn't.

The gray label on the box said the tape ran from July 2, 1968, through December 12, 1968. The librarian explained that the paper was a weekly, and that any event worth reporting that had happened during the week would be in the following week's edition. I pressed the FAST-FORWARD button, speeding the film to the week of October 10, figuring I would find what I was looking for there.

October 1968. I was eleven that year. We'd just left Newark heading to East Orange. Grandma had died. Maybe that was why I couldn't get her out of my mind. So much shit had gone down that year: Dr. King was killed. RFK gone a few months later. Looking through the days as they went past, courtesy of the pages on the microfiche, made me feel like a time traveler zapped back in time: Fresh whole chickens—29 cent a pound; Grand Union paper towels—three packages for a dollar. A short article, "Vietnam Yule Bags Filled," described how a local chapter of the Red Cross had been filling and packing Christmas sandwich bags for guys in Vietnam, and reminded me that Johnny had been there during the late 1960s. I'd almost forgotten. He'd been eighteen then. More pages whizzed by: Hospital expansion plans; local high school adding classes.

The boring, everyday details of life in a small Southern town. Nothing for the week of October 10. "Damn," I said aloud, and rolled to the next week, and then straight to the obits and read down quickly. Her name jumped out at me in boldface halfway down the page: WILLOW TURNER. A photograph of a young woman with dimples in her cheeks smiled back at me.

> Funeral services for Willow Turner, 26, were held Thursday at the Bynum Memorial Home. The Reverend Johnson Hayes officiated. Interment was in Glendale Cemetery.
>
> Born in Roanoke, Virginia, in 1942, Miss Turner had been a resident of Salem for twenty years. She recently suffered the death of her infant son, Terrell Curtis, 3 months old.
>
> Miss Turner is survived by her young daughter Willow, 6, and by an uncle, Dunbar Holt of Tampa, Florida.

No mention of the daughter's accidental killing of the son. No mention of the suicide. But what was I expecting? Young mother kills self in grief? Nobody talks about suicide; I knew that only too well.

I looked at the picture again, examining it for the resemblance that I knew must be there.

Willow Turner looked back at me, a gleam in her eyes and dimples in her cheeks, unaware that she would be dead by her own hand at age twenty-six.

It was her smile that told me, and I wondered how DeWayne could not have seen it, how he could have worked with July day in, day out, and not recognized Willow's smile. He didn't see it because he didn't want to. Had he packed that memory away where it wouldn't touch him? But then people see different things in other people. July's smile, those dimples creasing her cheeks, were what I'd noticed first about her, and they were here in this photo of her dead mother.

July. Willow's child.

July, who worked in DeWayne's office, and knew his habits and those of his sons. July knew Terrence and could get the keys to DeWayne's mother's home, who Hakim would believe had "something for him from his daddy." *The gun that shot DeWayne Junior would be the one that shot Hakim.*

I would have to get the report from Jenkins, put him in touch with Griffin and DeLorca. Do it fast. Because tomorrow was Sunday, and July was in Jersey and I was down here. *But why? Because she had killed her baby brother? Why?*

4:28. I glanced at the clock. It must be wrong. I stood up quickly, and the librarian glanced over at me, troubled, her eyes questioning if I would take the time to put the microfiche away, take the time to thank her. Do things that you're supposed to do in civilized places like libraries. But my heart was beating too fast to care. 4:29. How could I not have watched the time, lost track of minutes when there were so few of them?

I moved quickly, leaving the library without looking back. I stopped by the hotel to check out, pacing back and forth nervously as the clerk tallied up my charges and leisurely put them on my Amex card. It was 5:00. The plane left in twenty-eight minutes. *What would I do if I missed that plane?*

I pulled into the airport at 5:15 and jumped out of the car, running to the gate. But it was too late. The gate had closed. I cursed out everybody within hearing distance, saying things I knew I'd be ashamed of when I thought about it later, but I was mad and scared and those two things together made me into somebody I didn't want to be. When I'd finished, I sat down in one of the plastic seats in the far corner of the lobby, far away from the flight attendants who were getting ready to call security, and I cried.

I'd like to say some good-hearted older sister with kind eyes took my hand and snatched me back to reality. In my dreams. I had to do it myself. I finally pulled myself together, went into the ladies' room to wash my face, and made it over to the desk to ask the lady when

the next plane was leaving. She told me what
I already knew.

I drove back to the car rental place to tell
the guy I'd need to drive the car back to Newark. I was about four hundred and fifty miles
away, he told me, and I figured that it would
be about eight, eight and a half hours by car
if I drove straight through. It was going on
seven now. I could be home by three. Three
o'clock Sunday morning. I went back to the
restroom and changed from my suit into a pair
of sneakers, jeans and an oversized jacket,
which was comfortable for driving.

I would call Jake once I got on the road good
and tell him what I knew.

It will be all right, I told myself. I'd found out
what I'd come down here to find. Once I spoke
to Jake, spoke to Griffin, everything would be
all right.

Everything will be all right.

18

But it wasn't all right.

I'd stopped on the turnpike to try to call Jake, and then again after I'd been on the road for about an hour. It was eight-thirty by then. I tried paging Newark airport where I knew he would go to meet me, then I tried his place again. I finally called Phyllis's mother's place in Camden. Phyllis answered.

"What the fuck do you want with him?" she asked. I hadn't heard that tone in a while, that dead, suspicious voice that told me she was having one of her "spells," as Jake called them. My first reaction was sadness, then came the panic. Nothing I would say mean would anything to her, nothing would make any sense.

"Is Jake there?" I asked anyway.

"I get fucking tired of you always calling him at all hours of the day and night."

I paused and took a deep breath.

"Is Mrs. Williams there?" I asked, desperate to speak to her mother.

"No."

"Is she there in the house?"

Pause. "No. Get the fuck out of our lives."

"Phyllis," I said again, trying to reach her. "Please, if Jake calls—"

"He's not going to call."

"He's there?"

"I didn't say that." The voice was cagey, clever. But I knew he wasn't. I knew he had gone to meet me.

"Phyllis, I'm sorry," I muttered just before she hung up, and that was what I felt more than anything else. Sorry that she was back where she was, sorry that I was causing her pain. Sorry for me, for Jake, but mostly for her. I hung up myself and stood there for a minute. Then I tried to call DeWayne, then Griffin at home. DeWayne didn't answer. Griffin's machine was on, and I told him in the minute I had before the machine would cut off that July was the killer and that Jamal was with Jake. I managed to squeeze in Jake's address. Nothing. Not a goddamned thing. I slammed the phone back on the receiver, got back into the car and on the parkway.

I drove fast and angry, mulling over the whole thing—July, DeWayne and everything else that I'd found out—in my mind. I should have been glad that I'd figured the shit out, I guess, and maybe I would have, but all I felt was scared, scared and mad at myself for not seeing things clearer. I thought about Basil, and had second thoughts about the kitchen floor. I thought about how broke I always was and how dependent I was on DeWayne for the money he gave me every month. I had no business being dependent on him for shit. Damm, if my parents hadn't died and left me the house, I'd probably be homeless.

There's nowhere quite like a car for beating up on yourself. It's quiet, it's lonely and there's nobody to tell you to shut up and stop feeling sorry for yourself. Nothing but the road stretching long and lonely in front of you, and you on automatic pilot driving the miles away. So I beat myself up all the way to D.C.—about DeWayne, Basil and every mistake I'd made since junior high school. And then I figured I'd had enough.

It started to rain just as I entered Maryland, light at first and then heavy. Rain makes me sleepy, and the last thing I needed was to run into some damn truck. I had four or so more hours to go, and I'd never driven so far in one stretch like this; it was starting to get to me. I pulled into one of those gas and food drive-in places that dot the turnpike to get some coffee and something with a lot of sugar that would jolt me awake. It was midnight by then, and I was tired as hell.

The ladies' room was empty and kind of spooky, and I looked like death warmed over when I saw myself in the mirror. I spread some lipstick on my lips, which felt dry and chapped, and then thought how stupid it was to be putting it on at midnight in the bathroom, off the turnpike in the middle of nowhere. I decided I really was about to lose my mind. I splashed cold water on my face, dried it off with a paper towel and then went looking for something sweet.

I bought two fried apple pies and a large cup of black coffee with a couple of packets of what passed for cream. Then I sat down in a booth by the window so I wouldn't have to look at the aging truck driver who was slipping his tongue in and out of his mouth like that cretin in the truck who Thelma and Louise gave his just deserts. I cursed him out silently. He must be one desperate fool, I thought to myself. I looked almost as bad as the apple pie I had just bought tasted. I took another bite and followed it with a swallow of coffee that scalded my tongue as it went down my throat. But at least it woke me up.

I sat there sipping coffee and watching the rain drip down the window. I used to count raindrops when I was a kid, pretending that they were alive. I thought about that and about how it had been raining on my skylight the Sunday that DeWayne had first come by when everything had started, and that brought me back to Jamal, and a feeling of dread wrapped itself around me.

And then the guilt returned, for not knowing, for not protecting him like I should have, for not being there now. For being so wound up in my own pain, everything that I could never seem to get over in my life—Johnny's death, loneliness—that I hadn't seen July's weirdness for what it was.

I got up again, pushing those thoughts out of my mind; I went back to the phone and tried to get Jake again. Then I called the station for Griffin, and talked to a cop with a sleepy-sounding voice.

"It's an emergency. I have to talk to him tonight. Do you have a number where I can reach him? I tried him at home, I can't reach him there," I said.

"We don't give out that kind of information. Can I help you?"

I thought a minute. No. He couldn't help me. He wouldn't know what I was talking about. Griffin might not even know what I was talking about. I had to tell him myself.

"Ma'am, do you want to give me your name and where you can be reached?"

"I can't be reached," I said.

"Ma'am, I don't know how I can help you if you don't have a telephone number and an address." The irritation in his voice told me he was beginning to think I was a nut: Some crazy woman bugging one of his colleagues on a Saturday night. "You have to give me a telephone number, an address."

I thought for a minute, and then I gave him my telephone number and address at home and Jake's number.

"Can he reach you at these numbers now?"

"No, I should be there at three."

"Thank you, ma'am," he said. *Bring on the next nutcake, please,* I heard in his voice. "I'll see that Griffin gets the message," he said curtly, hanging up before I could add anything.

I cursed out loud, climbed back in the car and started driving. Through Maryland then over the Delaware bridge and past Delaware in half a minute. Into, out of Pennsylvania, onto the Jersey Turnpike, then the Garden State, finally to my block.

It was three o'clock and dead quiet when I finally got home. I sat in the car for a minute or two, my head slumped over the wheel, my hands sore and my back aching. I felt like somebody had whipped me, taken a stick and hit me like a dog until I couldn't do anything but cry. I don't know how long I sat there—two minutes or maybe ten, I just don't know. But then I got up and went into my house.

The phone was ringing as I was unlocking the door, and I dashed into the kitchen to answer it. Too late. It was probably Jake, I decided. Calling from Camden to see if I was back, worried because I'd missed the plane. I thought about calling him back, and then decided against it. He might be up, but his wife's family wasn't. Not at 3:15 A.M. on a Sunday morning. After that exchange with Phyllis, it was probably best to let things be.

I was back in town. Jamal was with Jake, probably asleep at his house, and he would bring him back tomorrow.

I turned on the faucet, let it run for a minute, and filled a glass full of water. I noticed that somebody had washed a saucer and two glasses and left them to drip dry on the dish rack. Jake and Jamal. They'd been here, either coming from or going to the airport. Someone had also left the peanut butter jar sitting on the counter with the top off—a sure sign of Jamal. And he was eating, another good sign. I chuckled to myself.

Everything was going to be all right.

I brought my bags in from the car, put on the teapot and sat down at the kitchen table. I thought about Basil. *Would I ever be able to enter this kitchen again without thinking about him?* The one good thing about all this was that I knew now that he was not guilty of this crime.

I poured some hot water over a Sleepytime teabag and glanced up at the clock. 3:20. I would call Griffin at eight. Jamal was with Jake. She couldn't get him.

3:30. I might as well stay up, I figured. Sit up, watch the sun rise. DeLorca would have to eat his words, wouldn't he? That was one pleasurable thought. Tamara Hayle, Private

Detective. *Saved your cop asses, didn't I?* I chuckled to myself.

Maybe I should call Jake. He had called me. He must be up. No. I'd have to be nuts calling folks at three thirty-five in the morning.

What then was this sense of dread? Why couldn't I shake it?

What harm would it do to call him? Jake would understand. God knows I'd called him at outrageous hours before. Not this outrageous. But late. Late enough for it to have become a part of his poor wife's madness.

I get fucking tired of you always calling us at all hours of the day and night.

She was right, as crazy as she was, she was right. But I needed him too. Or did I? My strength always surprised me.

3:45. *But maybe they weren't back in Camden. Maybe they were here. He knew how much I'd want to see Jamal. Why drive him back to Camden and then back here again?* He was probably at home on Springdale Avenue, fifteen minutes away. Of course. I picked up the phone and dialed his number. It rang, kept ringing.

OK. So much for that. He was back there in Camden, waiting to hear from me.

The phone rang. I jumped so high I had to laugh at myself as I reached to get it.

"Jake," I said, "I missed—"

"Tamara," the voice said, the soft, sane voice that belonged to Phyllis. "Tamara, is Jake there?"

"No," I said, trying to keep the panic out of my voice.

"He hasn't come home yet. I've been waiting for him."

"Did you give him the message?"

Pause. "What message? What are you talking about? He called at ten. He called from the house to say he was staying there. But I have to talk to him about something, Tamara. I can't sleep and I have to talk to him."

"Did you call him at home?"

"I can't get him. I've been calling and calling, but he won't answer the phone. What's wrong, Tamara, is he there? It's OK, if he's there. Please let me talk to him."

"He's not here, Phyllis," I said, and she began to cry.

My heart was in my throat now, so far up I felt I was choking. "When did he call you?" I asked, forgetting that she'd just told me.

"Ten."

My mind put the scene together. He'd come to pick me up at the airport. Him and Jamal. Maybe they'd gotten something to eat. Gone home then, waiting for me to call. That was probably when he called Phyllis.

"When was the last time you called him?" I asked her. But it didn't matter. I'd just called him myself. "I'll take care of it," I finally managed to say. "Don't worry, Phyl, I'll take care of it." I said it to her but I was talking to myself. I said it to keep cool, to get my heart back where it belonged. *Don't worry. I will take care of it. I will take care of it.*

I hung up and went upstairs to my bedroom and into the closet where I kept it. I loaded it quickly and slipped it into my pocket. Then I drove to Jake's house, where I knew I would find her.

19

"**Y**ou can come in now, Tamara. I know you're here," July said. I stopped dead, and then ran into the room where she was sitting, wondering what had given me away. I'd come into Jake's house through the basement, stealing up the stairs in my stocking feet like a kid playing hide-and-seek. I'd used the spare set of keys he kept in the gas grill in the backyard. I'd hoped to surprise her, give Jake enough time to jump her if she had a gun on him, because I knew if she hadn't killed them, she was holding them at gunpoint. But I was too late.

She had shot Jake. I heard the gun as I came up the last two stairs, and I'd run then, right to the door. But Jake had gambled and lost.

He was lying across the couch, blood oozing from a wound on his chest. I thought he was dead, and then he moaned, and I knew that he was alive, but I didn't know for how long.

Jamal sat next to him on the couch holding Jake's hand, too scared to cry.

She was sitting across from them in a cane-backed dining room chair that Jake had bought last year at IKEA. When I came into the room, I could see her reflection in the mirror over the couch. She could see me too.

She motioned for me to enter. She was pointing the gun at Jamal now, to make sure I'd obey her. I didn't let myself think about that gun or what it could do. I came in and stood within range of it.

"I know who you are now, Willow," I said. "That was your mother's name, wasn't it? Willow, like your mama." I made my voice matter-of-fact, sister-sweet. She looked at me, surprised, her mouth turned hard, then angry. But her eyes were steady and so was her hand.

"So you found out?" She smiled then, suddenly friendly, like this was the most natural thing in the world, and that scared the shit out of me.

I moved in a little, watching her, trying to read her mood, get a sense of what was in her mind. Then I smiled slowly.

"How did you know where to find them?" I asked. She smiled back, cunningly.

"I was waiting," she said simply. Not explaining.

"For me?"

"For him." She gestured toward Jamal with the gun and a chill went through me. I began to piece it together then, trying to think like she must have, figuring out what had happened. Jake must have gone to meet me at the airport. When I hadn't come, they'd gone back to the house, who knew why. Jamal had had something to eat, maybe they were waiting to hear from me, maybe just waiting for me to come. But she must have been waiting for him there. For how long, I wondered. An hour, two hours? Until midnight, on this fifth day, to come and claim her final victim? When she saw Jamal was with Jake, she must have laid in the cut, then followed them here, from my house. Had Jamal answered the door for her here, thinking it was me? Had Jake? I watched her, watched the gun.

"I just got back from Salem, from where you lived when you were a little girl," I said.

"I was never a little girl, Tamara." She cast her eyes down a moment and then back up, quickly. I believed her. She never had been a little girl.

"Don't make it any worse, July. What happened then is over. Don't make it any worse." But even as I said it, I was mouthing words to fill the silence and quell my fear. It couldn't get any worse. Too many were dead, and my son was next on her list. She had nothing to lose now, and she knew it.

"There's nothing you can do. I'm sorry, Tamara, but this is the way it has to be. It's the way things have to be."

"No they don't, Willow. Things don't have to go down like this. What about you after this? If you stop now, you can still . . ."

"I have nothing after this," she said with a resignation that told me she was telling me the truth as she saw it. "Nothing after this matters to me. If you went down there, you know what happened and you know what I have to do. And you know what I've already done." She nodded toward Jake. "It's too late. He tried to stop me, and I had to bring him into it. I'll have to bring you into it too. I don't have any choice."

I was shaking now but trying hard not to let her see it. *Never let an animal see you scared. It can smell fear like it can smell blood. Look it in the eye. Don't waver. Don't let it see your fear.* I didn't let July see mine. I looked her straight in the eye, not at the gun that was aimed at Jamal, not at Jake, who moaned on the couch beside him.

"Mommy?" Jamal said the word softly, pleading like it was a question. Not "Mom" or "Ma" like he called me. "Mommy," like he did when he was seven. *Mommy? What are you going to do?*

"Shut up, Jamal," I said it as hard and cold as I could, praying that he would know that I didn't mean it, that I had a reason for talking to him like that. I couldn't think of him now. He was alive and at this point that was as good as it got. It was between July and me. Willow and me.

If I could make her forget for a minute, and grab that moment to get the gun that felt heavy in the pocket of my jacket, I could use it. I would have to be quick and train everything I had on it because there would be just one moment, I knew that, and that was the only chance we had.

"How did you know I was here?" she asked, distracting me. I couldn't let that happen again.

"I didn't," I answered nonchalantly, watching her eyes. "I came by to get my son."

"At four in the morning?" She looked at me incredulously, laughing at me. I kept my eyes glued to hers.

"Well, I admit," I said, with fake charm, "it's a little late, but the plane was late, and I knew he was here, and we"—I pointed toward Jake—"we have an arrangement." If I could make her remember those few times we'd bonded—at my house that time when she'd brought the letter from the ME about Terrence, Thursday night at Hakim's wake—maybe I could touch her. Maybe it wouldn't have to be played out until one of us was dead.

"Don't play me cheap, Tamara," July said. "Please don't play me cheap." Her eyes were telling me that she was not a fool, and that whatever bonding we'd done wasn't enough to pull us through this.

"You're right," I said. "I knew you were here. Why don't you just give it up. The cops know what has gone down. It's over, July, Willow, whatever you want to call yourself. Just give it up."

"The cops don't know shit, you know that as well as I do and you know my real name now. You know what happened."

Wrong move. She turned serious, deadly serious, her eyes flashed angrily. "Sit down," she said, gesturing toward the end of the couch near Jamal. I sat down cautiously, knowing that would make it harder to get the gun when I got that moment.

"There," she said, pointing closer to Jamal as if she could read my mind. "And take it off."

"Take what off?" I played dumb.

"The damn jacket," she said impatiently.

"I'm cold."

"Bring it here. The jacket, bring it over."

My breath caught in my throat, but I smiled at her. "Sure," I said figuring out my options, which were nil. I brought it to her, and she shook it with one hand, banging it against the edge of her chair. The gun hit the wood with a dull thud.

"I'm cold," she said, mocking me with a nasty sneer.

"What did you expect?"

"More from you. So you knew I was here?"
She went back to what I said.

"Yeah."

"Then you know why I'm here."

I didn't answer, but forced myself to stare
her down, like kids do seeing who'll blink
first. I could feel Jamal's knee trembling
against mine.

Somewhere in the back of the house, a ra-
diator hissed softly, and the furnace rumbled
loudly in the basement. Everyday noises. Jake
stirred and then moaned. I yearned to touch
him, to comfort him.

"Mommy," Jamal asked, defying my unspoken order. "Can I get Jake some water, please
can I get him some water?"

"You get it," July said, pointing to me.
"You, Jamal, come over here." He glanced at
me, and I nodded for him to obey, and he war-
ily approached her, standing as far away from
her as he could, as she held the gun at his
head.

Blood was still coming from Jake's wound,
more slowly now, and his moans were fainter.
I got the water quickly, running the tap water
fast, not waiting for it to get cold, and brought
it back to him, gently picking his head up to
take a sip. He opened his eyes slightly. "You'll
be OK," I mouthed to him silently. "You'll be
OK." I touched the side of his cheek, feeling
his rough beard against the palm of my hand
and then touched his lips with my fingertips.

We both knew that something would have to happen fast if he was going to make it.

"Sit back down," she ordered. Jamal came and sat back down beside me.

"It's almost time," she said finally, shifting slightly in her chair, but never letting the gun move or taking her eyes from me.

From the moment that she'd shot Jake until now, I'd wondered what she was waiting for, why she hadn't finished him off, shot Jamal since it was Sunday, shot me when I'd first come in. What the fuck was she waiting for? *Time for what?*

"Time?" I asked.

"First light," she said solemnly. "I'm waiting for first light." We both glanced out the window, almost at the same time, and then back quickly at each other, her in anticipation, me in fear. "I swore to myself when I started this whole thing that the last one would die at dawn of day on Sunday, the fifth day, and that's almost now," she said. "When dawn comes, at first light."

What time was it now, four-thirty? Four-forty-five? When would dawn come? I couldn't remember. How much time did we have?

Could I keep her talking? I thought about Griffin. Maybe he had gotten the message. And maybe he was heading out the door right now, down the road, and would barrel into this room with guns drawn like somebody on

TV. Or maybe I would get that moment I was waiting for. But the damn gun was over near her foot. It would take more than a minute. Two minutes. Three minutes, if I were lucky. Prayers were all I had. I managed to find my voice, but there was a cold knot of fear in the pit of my stomach.

"July, could you tell me something?" I spoke to her quietly, intimately. "Why did you start all this?"

She smiled. "It happened by chance."

"By chance?"

"It started with my uncle." She paused slightly, her lips pursing, almost as if she had just bitten into something bitter.

"Your uncle Holt," I said, remembering his name from the article in the paper.

"Yes," she said. She looked distracted for a moment. "He died. My uncle died, and I had to go back there, back to where it happened, back to Salem to find out about my mother. I ran into him at a club. We got to talking. He said his name. Just by chance."

I knew who "he" was. "DeWayne Jr.?"

"And it all came back," she continued, without answering my question and with wonder in her voice as if she were just understanding it herself for the first time. "Just hearing his name, DeWayne's name, brought it all back."

"And it was October," I added, knowing now that her brother had died then and later her mother.

"Yes," she said quickly, searching my eyes. "And it was October."

"And DeWayne Jr. told you where to find his father," I continued filling in the blanks.

"I got it out of him, and then I shot him two days later." She said it matter-of-factly, the words and her tone of voice making me shiver involuntarily. I tensed my body, arming myself against feeling or vulnerability.

"And then you came up here?" I asked, finding my voice.

"No, I went back down there first, down to Florida. I had some things to get," she added, her voice suddenly hushed, almost a whisper, and for a moment there was panic in her eyes, a fear that seemed to come from the bottom of her soul. She glanced from me over to the window, her body tense. I wondered why.

"Why did you go back down there?"

"Because there were things I had to get," she said to me, glancing at me impatiently, repeating herself.

"What things?"

"Things to kill a man so nobody will know you've done it, with seeds that don't grow here," she said, her voice mocking me.

"Is that what you mixed with the cocaine to kill Terrence?" She looked at me, her eyebrow cocked slightly in surprise.

"Yeah. He'd called his daddy to ask for some money, said he had the flu. I told

278

DeWayne I'd take the money by . . . and the capsules I fixed."

"You came to see him the day he died?"

"The day before. I knew he'd take them sooner or later, in time to die on time."

"You sent the flowers?"

"Why the hell would I send him flowers? His mama did. That's what he told me, anyway. He was mad as hell, and he said his mama had sent him these damn flowers, and they were making him sneeze and she should have known better, and he threw them in the trash when I was there. I gave him the pills then and told him they would take care of the sneezing and his cold, too. Cured him of all his ills, didn't they?" she added with a chuckle, the wisecracking July for a moment.

"When Carlotta gave you back the keys to DeWayne's mother's place after she had her sets made, you had a set made for yourself, too," I said, knowing that was the way it had gone down.

"That little whore was with him every Thursday night. Stupid whore. Every Thursday night. They never went into the basement. I sat down there until she left. I heard the water running loud through the pipes, the shower was broke, knew he was probably taking a bath, high. I just drowned him, like you do a cat."

"Why did there have to be five days between them?" I asked, softly, patiently, like I was a teacher prodding a reluctant kid for answers I knew she had. "Between Terrence and Gerard and . . ." I couldn't say the last one; the words wouldn't come out.

"Because there were five days between them, my brother's and my mother's death. That was how it worked out. That was how I made it work out," she answered like a reluctant kid, with a slight smile, proud to know the answer.

Jamal's breath came short and tight, and I took his hand for a moment, squeezing it gentle. I knew that in his mind he had asked her about Hakim and had heard her answer. We both knew now who was driving that red car. We knew that the gun she was holding had killed his brother. He didn't wipe away the tears that rolled down his face; I don't think he even felt them. I glanced over at Jake. His breath was shallow now and so faint I could hardly hear it.

She changed hands, holding the gun in the right. She rubbed the sweat off the left one and I noticed again the missing ends of her fingers, the first thing I'd noticed that day when I saw her in DeWayne's office, the thing about herself she'd tried so hard to hide.

"He took them in pieces," she said suddenly, gesturing with her chin down to her deformed fingers. She said it matter-of-factly, informatively as if she had no more secrets to hide. It took me by surprise, and for a moment

I didn't know what she was talking about, but then my eyes followed hers down to the hand that was balled into a fist. She spoke in a whisper now, talking more to herself than to me, and I strained to hear her. "They said I killed my baby brother and my mama, and I was evil to the core. Whenever I cried for Mama who shamed them, he took little bits of them in pieces."

"Who?"

"My uncle Holt," she said.

My hand went to my mouth, shutting out my involuntary gasp of horror. I knew the truth now, of what had made Willow's child July. She had left her dead mother to find her fate south of Tampa, and that fate had killed her soul. Had they cut her to teach her a lesson—from rage, from hate? I wondered. She shifted her eyes quickly away from mine in shame as she had the first time I saw her.

"It's time," she said, standing up suddenly, moving away from the high-backed chair toward us, killing the thought of them, of what she had run from.

Jamal's eyes were wide now, from her story and what he had seen. I felt him stiffen as his eyes sought mine. *What are you going to do?* they asked me. *What are you going to do?*

She'll have to come through me before she gets to you, I answered him in my heart. It was the one truth I knew. But had that moment when she let her guard down come and gone?

"It's not dawn yet," I said to her. I stood up now too, moving forward toward her, away from the couch. She stood her ground.

"It soon will be."

The air was still, Jamal's fear palpable, almost like an odor. Jake's breathing had become more labored, frightening me. My heart beat so hard in my chest I could hear it in my ears.

"Do you remember what happened that day, July?" I asked it recklessly, with no thought of the consequences or what taking her that far back would do. There was a twitch at the corner of her mouth. I'd touched something deep. I pushed on. "Do you remember what you were doing when it happened? How you dropped him? How it sounded when he hit the floor?" I said it maliciously, bullying her, like a kid teasing someone who can be taunted until she wets her pants.

Her eyes went dead for a moment, and then a look of anguish came into them I will remember until my dying day.

"*He* dropped him," she said in a small voice mixed with wonder and fear. "He dropped the baby. Terrell reached to get my cookie. He couldn't hold Terrell because he was wet; babies are slippery when they're wet. He didn't know that? He couldn't hold him? He had to *drop* him on the floor?" She asked the questions like a kid, looking up to me as if she expected me to answer her. "*He* dropped him.

282

He told them I did it, but he did it. He did it. I had to pay him back. I had to pay him back for what he did to us."

What DeWayne had done to her mother, who killed herself. Her brother, whom he'd killed. To her, whom he had sent to hell.

She stood there, immobilized by what she had said, and in that moment I lunged toward her, knocking her back against the chair. She glanced up at me, a question in her eyes that were wide now in surprise, as she fell backward. The gun she was holding went off over our heads, the bullet hitting a far wall. The sound of it shattered the silence and startled us both.

"Damn you," she spat at me as she aimed the gun at me, but I moved fast, charging her and knocking it from her hand; it skittered across the floor like a leaden animal. We both dove for it, knocking each other out of the way, scrambling together in the tight space between the chair and the couch on the rug, the dust and a whiff of Samsara going up my nose.

"Run, Jamal, run," I screamed as I moved, and he scrambled, head first, over the back of the couch onto the floor and nearly into the wall behind it. But in the second that it had taken me to look and scream, she had the advantage, and used it before I could move. She was stronger, bigger than me, and she reached for the gun that had fallen, grabbing it from my hand, pushing me out of the way with her arm and then aiming for Jamal. He moved quickly, scrambling along the floor toward the kitchen. The shot she fired at him hit the wall and shattered the plaster as he ducked behind the door. She rose, heading toward him, stalking him. I froze as I watched her get up, froze as I saw the door he was behind move as he pushed his body further into the wall trying to hide from her. She shot again, and he screamed out in fear. In that second, I saw it out of the corner of my eye, lying where she'd left it on the floor. I reached for it, fast into the pocket, aimed and fired it in one perfect, fluid motion. She turned and looked at me with eyes that couldn't see, and then fell back, the bullet leaving a hole the size of a dime in the middle of her forehead.

I don't remember too much about what happened after that. Jamal called the police. Griffin came. I started praying. I found out that Jake would be OK. But two thoughts stayed with me, through the cops, the questions, the sirens that sounded: That DeWayne was the one who had killed the baby, and that I had just killed the sister.

EPILOGUE

"**W**hat the hell else can I say except I'm sorry? If I could change things, if I could bring that baby back, don't you think I would? Do you despise me that much?" His voice cracked as he spoke, and his eyes searched mine for something I couldn't give him.

"I don't despise you, DeWayne," I said. "Despite what you may think, I don't despise you." I looked at him blankly, with no emotion, then stared past him and the pot of tea we were sharing, outside the kitchen window to the tree that looked like it was dying.

When Jamal had heard that DeWayne was coming, his mouth had tightened into a hard, thin line. "I hate that lying son of a bitch," he'd said.

"He's your father," I reminded him. "Don't curse your father."

"I don't have a father."

"Don't say that."

"There's nothing you can say to change my mind," he'd said evenly, and then he'd left through the back door, his body tense and his hands balled into fists. I didn't say anything to him about it then or to DeWayne when he came inside later. He'd lost all his sons now, even mine, and I didn't see any sense in telling him something he already knew.

I shifted my eyes from the tree back to DeWayne, whose eyes were moist.

"It became a part of me after a while, Tammy, like a cut or a deep scratch that turns into a scar." He paused for a moment, searching my eyes again. "You want to hear what happened?"

"It's done now." I was tired of everything, and I just wanted him to go home. "It's over, DeWayne. You have to go on with your life the best you can." The words were empty clichés and I knew it, but I couldn't think of anything better to say.

"Do you think I meant to kill that boy? My own son?" The anger made his voice high, and it shook uncontrollably, but the rage wasn't directed at me so I didn't take it personally. "Did she really think I meant to do it?"

"She was a little girl," I finally said. "Nobody knows what she thought."

"She was six and I was twenty-one. I didn't even know she was in the room when I told them, for Christ's sake. They would have tried me for manslaughter, Tammy. I would have spent ten good years of my life in jail. They didn't care nothing about no justice for a black man, but a little girl? They'd forgive her, coddle her, feel sorry for her. Go out of their way to see that nobody even mentioned it. I figured she'd probably never even know I'd told them she did it. Who would mention something like that to a child? How could I know her mama was going to take it like she did? How was I supposed to know that?"

"You never know what will happen in life," I said. *More clichés, more bullshit.* "You make your choices, and I guess you have to live with them."

"Will Jamal ever forgive me?" he said, his eyes frightened for the first time that morning.

"Can you forgive yourself?" I asked.

He didn't answer, he just sat there looking at that dead tree like I had and after a few more minutes he left.

November is not good for a hell of a lot besides Thanksgiving, and it was the Sunday after that I finally made my way to her grave. Jake had told me that I didn't owe her shit, and I knew I didn't, but I couldn't let it go. They never tell you how hard it is to kill another person, how it messes with you, even when it goes down like it did between me and July. It was a blot on my soul, and I knew it. A wound that would have to grow into a scar the way DeWayne said his did, and I'd have to live with that scar the same way he had.

The City buried her. I had to bribe a clerk at the morgue to find out where. It was sunny the day I went, warmer than it had been in a month. I bought some roses at the Pathmark, eight bucks for half a dozen red ones. She'd told me once that she knew she'd never have a funeral and I'd told her that she would. So I stood where they said they put her, and dropped six roses, one by one, on her lonely, unmarked grave. Then I said a prayer, asking for salvation and strength to heal my spirit and that of my son.

"So you're Tamara Hayle," said the tall, gaunt man who walked into my office without knocking. "DeLorca says you're the best P.I. in Essex County. I only do business with the best." He had flawless dark skin, thick silver-gray hair, and was dressed like a banker in a navy pin-striped suit and black wing-tipped shoes. But he had the dead eyes of a street thug. *Killer's eyes*, I thought to myself, even though I knew better.

Lincoln E. Storey was a legend in Newark, and I wondered why the photos that always ran in *Black Enterprise* and on the business pages of *The Star-Ledger* never captured the predatory glint in his eyes. I also wondered why DeLorca, chief of the Belvington Heights police force and my grumpy ex-boss, had given me such a sparkling endorsement.

"Yes, I'm Tamara Hayle. Would you like to sit down?" I asked, extending a hand. He glanced at my offering but didn't take it. I reached for his overcoat, a dove-gray cashmere number that felt as soft as mink against my palm, and hung it up on the rocky coatrack in a dark corner of my office.

"I assume you know who I am," he said with an arrogant thrust of his chin.

"Is there anyone in the state of New Jersey who doesn't?" I hated the ingratiating sound of my voice, but it was too late to call it back. "What can I do for you, Mr. Storey?" I asked, trying hard to tone down my eagerness.

"I'll get to that," he snapped in a way that told me he was a man who was used to taking his own time and getting his own way. His tone caught me short, but I tossed him a sugary smile, deciding in that instant to listen to my pocketbook rather than my pride.

For "the best P.I. in Essex County," I was as broke as hell. With a 1982 diesel Jetta that needed a new transmisison and a big-mouthed teenage son to feed, being anything but pleasant to the biggest client who had ever graced my funky little office would be just plain foolish.

Spring had touched everything in Newark but me. The cherry trees were blossoming in Weequahic and Branch Brook Parks, and folks, sick and tired of the Hawk and the harshest winter in fifteen years, were stepping out into the sun. My best friend, Annie, had fallen in love with her husband of the last ten years . . .

again. After the worst year of his young life, my son Jamal had beaten down grief and discovered, with a vengeance, the opposite sex. And Wyvetta Green, the owner of Jan's Beauty Biscuit, the beauty salon downstairs, who I could always count on for a sweet spirit and sour words, had dyed her hair a hot-to-trot blond and was planning a week in Jamaica with her gold-toothed boyfriend, Earl. But I was horny *and* broke, and I couldn't think of two worst things to be in spring which, up until this year, had always been my favorite season. It didn't bode well for the rest of the year. I'd been sitting at my desk, lamenting my sorry state, when Lincoln E. Storey had walked through my door. I wasn't about to let him walk out.

"Could I get you something to drink, Mr. Storey?" I asked. "A cup of tea?"

"I don't drink tea."

"How about some coffee?"

"Freshly-brewed?"

"Sorry, I don't have a pot. Instant okay?" I asked. I don't like instant, but I keep it in my office to be polite.

"I don't drink that shit."

That "shit" business threw me for a minute, but I swallowed the urge to tell him to kiss my behind and watched him as he crossed his long legs and surveyed, I feared, the second-hand computer that separated us, the film on the window that dimmed the sun, and the streak of brown gravy that had found its way to the front of my blouse when I'd shared some egg foo young with Wyvetta at lunch. I also recalled the first time I'd seen him.

I was twelve years old then, one of maybe three hundred bored kids assembled in our junior high auditorium to honor him on Black Heroes Day. Lincoln E. Storey, a local boy made good, had grown up on the mean streets of the toughest ward in Newark and made money's mama as one of the first black investment bankers on Wall Street. He was, as the principal told us in a flowery introduction, a young man who had studied hard, paid his dues, and made his dreams come true.

This was the late 1960s then, a time for dreams and nightmares, too. The flames of the riot in '67 had charred the city's soul as hard as burnt wood. Everybody was looking for a hero, and Storey was made to order. He was in his twenties then, old by our standards. He'd stood tall and stern in his charcoal gray suit and explained the market and how he'd learned to work it, and how if we studied hard, we could learn to work it, too. We didn't understand the market, but we understood rich and the reverent, shy posturing of our principal and teachers, who gathered like spring hens around a young cock.

But later that night when I'd mentioned Storey to my father, his eyes had hardened.

"I remember Lincoln, Seafus Storey's boy,"

he'd said. "He lived in that dilapidated old tenement over there on Irvine Turner Boulevard, just off Avon, back in the days when Turner Boulevard was Belmont, before the big-time Negroes took over City Hall. His daddy used to whip that boy all up and down the avenue every time the mood hit him good. I always wondered what became of him."

I remembered my father's eyes as I watched Storey now, and wondered how old he had been when the cruel lines around his mouth had settled in his face as deeply as dimples.

"How long have you been in this business?" Storey asked, snapping me from my memories.

"Five years going on six."

"You're licensed by the state?"

"Of course."

"What kind of things do you handle?"

"Anything that comes my way. Disappearances. Missing persons. Occasionally the public defender will ask me to help on a homicide or larceny. Insurance fraud."

"And your rates?"

"Depends on the job, plus all my expenses."

"And you're worth the money?"

"That's what they tell me."

"Do you find this line of work hard for a woman, a black woman?"

"No harder than being a cop."

"You used to work for DeLorca, I take it."

"Six years ago."

"Why did you leave?"

"I got sick of it," I said, wondering how much DeLorca had told him about me.

"Sick of . . ."

"Sick of being called a nigger bitch every day of my beat," I said, the old anger surfacing again, coloring the edge of my words. Storey chuckled deep in his throat, and our eyes locked for a moment, telling me he hadn't forgotten his roots. "So I take it you live in Belvington Heights?" I asked, knowing the answer, but tired of responding to his questions.

"You grew up around here?" he asked, changing the subject. His thin hand swept elegantly toward the window indicating that "around here" meant Main Street, East Orange, Newark, and beyond.

"East Orange. Newark. The same ward as you."

A glint of something I couldn't read came and left his eyes.

"Discretion means as much to me as money," he said out of nowhere.

"I know how to keep my mouth shut."

"You do surveillance work?"

"I've done it."

"You like it?"

"It depends."

"On?"

"On who I'm following and where they lead me."

He smiled a crooked smile that told me nothing. "I need to get some . . . information on somebody." He paused. "I need to know every bit of shit about this motherfucking cocksucker that I can possibly get. Do you understand me?"

It wasn't the words that got me. I've heard men curse before. My dead brother, Johnny, could belt them out harder than anybody I ever knew. But the way Storey's face broke when he spoke, the way he lost control and his lower lip trembled and his eyes squinted, was downright scary. Whoever the "motherfucking cocksucker" was, he had made Storey's shit list big time.

"Is this person an employee?" I asked neutrally, cooling my voice against the heat I heard in his.

Storey smirked. "You could say that, I guess, depending upon how you define employee."

He was being cagey, and I wondered why he wasn't giving it to me straight.

"I take it this is somebody who has betrayed your trust?" I asked, stating the obvious.

"I want to know where he sleeps and who he fucks," he answered bluntly.

"Does he sleep with someone you know?" I asked innocently, making my voice sound caring, sister-gentle, willing to share a brother's pain. *Somebody you sleep with?* I didn't ask.

He straightened his back, uncrossing his

legs, and folded his hands. "My stepdaughter," he said after a minute. "I assume they're sleeping together. My stepdaughter, Alexa, is involved with this person, this character. I don't trust him. I suspect he likes my money more than he likes my stepdaughter. I want to find out everything I can about him."

"So what's his name?" I asked.

"Brandon Pike."

"Brandon Pike," I uttered the name once softly to myself, like I'd never heard it before. But it had hit me like a fast, hard punch in the gut—lower, because when I had known and loved him, that was where Brandon Pike had hurt me—my female center, the most vulnerable part of me.

Lincoln Storey studied my face, taking in the change that I knew was there.

"You know him then?" He watched my eyes as they dropped. I forced them back up, confronting his.

"Years ago. . . Not well."

Storey seemed to buy it.

"He has been seeing Alexa for about a year. She's twenty-three. Dropped out of school in upstate New York. Vassar. Trying to find herself. He's—how old would you say—in his thirties? He's come into her life. After my money, anyone can tell that. She's got nothing to offer him. He's that kind of man. My wife, Daphne, and I are very concerned." His eyes sought mine for a reaction, and then he continued. "If I can get something on him, I can confront her with it. It's clear she has nothing to give him."

What is he giving her? I asked myself, because that had been Brandon's special talent: giving women what they thought they needed.

I had spent the years after our affair trying to figure him out. And all I really knew in the end was that I'd left my joke of a marriage to my ex, DeWayne Curtis, with my head high, and Brandon Pike had brought it low, lower than I'd ever let it fall for any man again.

"I want you to follow him. Find out what you can on him. See what he's up to. Report it to me," Storey continued.

I wondered for a moment if getting into Brandon's business was really an ethical thing for me to do. Was it right to use my professional skills to take an assignment to get even with somebody who had done me wrong? P.I.s are supposed to be objective, removed from the subject. Cool, detached. I wondered if I could be that way where Brandon Pike was concerned. But it had been three years since he'd left me—me wondering what I'd done wrong and if I'd failed him. He'd severed everything then. Professionally. Personally. Permanently.

And ethics aside, I truly needed the money. And on the real tip, the son of a bitch deserved it.

"What you can tell me about him now? I'll

need a recent photo, current home address, work address?" I asked, slipping into my professional mode again, pushing back the personal.

Storey looked at me blankly.

"I know that he got an award a couple of years ago for *Slangin' Rock*, the documentary he did on kids dealing cocaine. Is he making any money yet? Is he still doing docs?" I asked.

"I thought you didn't know him well."

"I haven't seen him in about five years," I said, looking Storey in the eye. *Three years*.

"Do you have a recent photo?" I asked again. Maybe he *had* changed in three years.

"Why the hell would I carry around a photograph of Brandon Pike?"

"Why the hell would you come to my office wanting me to tail somebody and not have a picture of him," I snapped back, deciding in that flash of a moment that maybe I didn't need Lincoln Storey's money after all, not bad enough anyway to put up with his attitude. Not bad enough to risk raking up the embers of Brandon Pike.

Storey smiled what he probably thought was a charming smile. "I like a woman with spirit," he said.

"Mr. Storey, don't waste my time." Suddenly I was as sick of him as I'd ever been of anybody in my life.

"No. To answer your question, I don't have

any photographs. And I can't tell you a lot about him because I don't know anything or I wouldn't be hiring you. But I'm giving a fundraiser tonight for Stella Pharr. Stella Pharr."

"Tonight?"

"Yes, for Stella Pharr," he repeated for the third time.

"Stella Pharr?" I asked. I'd heard the name before but couldn't place it, Storey seemed to relish the sound of it.

"Yes. Deputy district attorney. She's running for state assembly. Alexa, my wife, Daphne, Pike. They'll all be there. At Tate's. You know Tate's used to be on West Market. Now it's on Fullbright in Belvington Heights."

"Yes, I know the place." Jackson Tate's ancient, elfin face quickly came to mind. Tate's had been the hottest new restaurant in the comeback of Newark. Tate had raised hackles and eyebrows all over town when he'd moved it to Belvington Heights, which needed another ritzy restaurant like another Lexus dealership. My friend, Jake, who loves Newark more than anyone else I know, had been particularly pissed off, despite the fact that he'd briefly worked for Tate as a maitre'd when he was in law school, and loved Tate's apple pie as much as I did. He hadn't eaten in the new location since it opened.

Jackson Tate had grown to manhood with my father on Howard Street, a cobblestoned stretch of rowhouses, when it was one of the saddest streets in town. It's all gone now, along with the despair that marked it. I remembered the birthday cakes Tate used to make me and his rolls—"floating light" my daddy used to call them. And I remembered Tate's dream of starting a restaurant: a young man's fantasy come true in old age. But I'd been to Tate's only once since he'd moved to Belvington Heights; his price range was definitely out of mine.

"How much are the tickets?" I asked, wondering if I had the price of entry.

"Two hundred and fifty dollars apiece, but you won't have to pay," Storey said, as if he were reading my mind. "Bring a friend if you want. I'll tell Tate to bill me. I own him."

"You own Tate?" I asked, not disguising the surprised disgust in my voice.

But Storey didn't seem to hear it. He reached into his suit pocket, took out an ivory-colored card with his name and address on it, then a checkbook, and scribbled out a check. I glanced at the card before stuffing it and the check into a slot of my worn gray wallet, my heart skipping a beat as I noticed the one and three loopy zeroes scratched with the tip of his Mont Blanc fountain pen.

"Under no circumstances do I want my wife or stepdaughter to know anything about all this." He paused. "For obvious reasons."

"Obvious reasons?" I could understand his stepdaughter, but not his wife.

"Clearly the less Alexa knows, the less she'll share with Pike. I don't want to worry Daphne. She has enough on her mind as is." His eyes shifted away from mine. I wondered if he was lying. Even if he was, I decided it wasn't my business.

"Okay," I said. "As I said before, I know how to keep my mouth shut."

"Get to Tate's before nine. There may not be too much of a crowd then, and you won't have any trouble finding us. Watch Pike carefully. See who he talks to, watch what he does. I'll see you tonight?" he asked, suddenly anxious.

I glanced at my watch. It was four-thirty, but the bank was open late so I figured I'd have time to scoot by there, deposit the check, and pick up a pizza at Pizza Hut for Jamal before he cleaned out the refrigerator. I'd also call Annie and see if she could pull herself away from William long enough to hang out at Tate's tonight. I figured she would. She liked good food almost as much as she liked her old man, and Tate's still had some of the best food in Essex County.

"Tonight is fine," I said smiling my sweet professional smile. But two questions lingered in my mind: how had Storey gotten a piece of Tate and did I *really* want to know who Brandon was sleeping with?

I let them rest, though. Storey's check was already burning a hole in my pocket.

"Thank you, Mr. Storey," I said.

"I think we can do business together, Ms. Hayle."

As he reached for his coat off the rack and turned to leave, a sharp, hard rap on the door drew our attention.

"You in there, Tamara?" It was Wyvetta, jiggling the knob on my door. "I still got some of those egg rolls left over from lunch if you want to take them home to Jamal."

"Wyvetta, I have somebody in here with me. A client!" I added firmly, but not quickly enough to head her off. Wyvetta, grinning and waving a greasy bag from the Golden Dragon, barged through the door.

"Oh, girl, I'm sorry . . . " she said as soon as she spotted Lincoln Storey, but just as quickly the smile dropped from her face.

Storey, with a look that could have turned hell cold, stepped away from both of us, his eyes darting nervously to Wyvetta, then back to me, and finally settling on Wyvetta. "Please excuse me, ladies," he sputtered, sweeping his dove-gray coat over his shoulders, and nearly knocking me over in his rush to get out the door.

"Wyvetta, do you know—"

"Yeah, I know him, Wyvetta said, cutting me off, her eyes filled with contempt. "I know him better than he thinks." She spat twice like a cat, in the path Storey had cut, and her spit spread in a thin, nasty line down the hall.

FAST-PACED MYSTERIES
BY J.A. JANCE

Featuring J.P. Beaumont

UNTIL PROVEN GUILTY	89638-9/$4.99 US/$5.99 CAN
INJUSTICE FOR ALL	89641-9/$4.50 US/$5.50 CAN
TRIAL BY FURY	75138-0/$4.99 US/$5.99 CAN
TAKING THE FIFTH	75139-9/$4.99 US/$5.99 CAN
IMPROBABLE CAUSE	75412-6/$4.99 US/$5.99 CAN
A MORE PERFECT UNION	75413-4/$4.99 US/$5.99 CAN
DISMISSED WITH PREJUDICE	
	75547-5/$4.99 US/$5.99 CAN
MINOR IN POSSESSION	75546-7/$4.99 US/$5.99 CAN
PAYMENT IN KIND	75836-9/$4.99 US/$5.99 CAN
WITHOUT DUE PROCESS	75837-7/$4.99 US/$5.99 CAN
FAILURE TO APPEAR	75839-3/$5.50 US/$6.50 CAN

Featuring Joanna Brady

DESERT HEAT	76545-4/$4.99 US/$5.99 CAN
TOMBSTONE COURAGE	76546-2/$5.99 US/$6.99 CAN

Buy these books at your local bookstore or use this coupon for ordering:

Mail to: Avon Books, Dept BP, Box 767, Rte 2, Dresden, TN 38225   C
Please send me the book(s) I have checked above.
❏ My check or money order— no cash or CODs please— for $_____is enclosed
(please add $1.50 to cover postage and handling for each book ordered— Canadian residents add 7% GST).
❏ Charge my VISA/MC Acct#_____Exp Date_____
Minimum credit card order is two books or $6.00 (please add postage and handling charge of $1.50 per book — Canadian residents add 7% GST). For faster service, call 1-800-762-0779. Residents of Tennessee, please call 1-800-633-1607. Prices and numbers are subject to change without notice. Please allow six to eight weeks for delivery.

Name_____
Address_____
City_____State/Zip_____
Telephone No._____   JAN 0395